SCIENCE FICTION GEMS

Volume 2

James Blish
and others

I0532656

ARMCHAIR FICTION
PO Box 4369, Medford, Oregon 97504

For more information about Armchair Books and products, visit our website at…

www.armchairfiction.com

Or email us at…

armchairfiction@yahoo.com

TALES OF YESTERDAY'S TOMORROW...

"King of the Hill" and "Journey for the Brave" take you deep into the human subconscious...a frightening place to be when alone for too long.

"The Guest Rites" chronicles the futuristic tale of patient aliens and a human criminal, while the Hugo nominated "Rat in the Skull" offers a different view about animal intelligence.

"The Marching Morons" and "Never Gut-Shoot a Wampus" makes it clear that even in the future money and power cannot buy you brains...

Here is another exciting collection of great sci-fi authors from the past. Rocket, super-sled, or teleport yourself to worlds and adventures aplenty!

TABLE OF CONTENTS

Rat in the Skull

By ROG PHILLIPS

Some people will be shocked by this story. Others will be deeply moved.
Everyone who reads it will be talking about it.
Read the first four pages: then put it down if you can.

DR. JOSEPH MacNare was not the sort of person one would expect him to be in the light of what happened. Indeed, it is safe to say that until the summer of 1955 he was more "normal", better adjusted, than the average college professor. And we have every reason to believe that he remained so, in spite of having stepped out of his chosen field.

At the age of thirty-four, he had to his credit a college textbook on advanced calculus, an introductory physics, and seventy-two papers that had appeared in various journals, copies of which were in neat order in a special section of the bookcase in his office at the university, and duplicate copies of which were in equally neat order in his office at home. None of these were in the field of psychology, the field in which he was shortly to become famous—or infamous. But anyone who studies the published writings of Dr. MacNare must inevitably conclude that he was a competent, responsible scientist, and a firm believer in institutional research, research by teams, rather than in private research and go-it alone secrecy, the course he eventually followed.

In fact, there is every reason to believe he followed this course with the greatest of reluctance, aware of its pitfalls, and that he took every precaution that was humanly possible.

Certainly, on that day in late August, 1955, at the little cabin on the Russian River, a hundred miles upstate from the university, when Dr. MacNare completed his paper on *An Experimental Approach to the Psychological Phenomena of Verification,* he had no slightest thought of "going it alone."

It was mid-afternoon. His wife, Alice, was dozing on the small dock that stretched out into the water, her slim figure tanned a smooth brown that was just a shade lighter than her hair. Their eight-year-old son, Paul, was fifty yards upstream playing with some other boys, their shouts the only sound except for the whisper of rushing water and the sound of wind in the trees.

Dr. MacNare, in swim trunks, his lean muscular body hardly tanned at all, emerged from the cabin and came out on the dock.

"Wake up, Alice," he said, nudging her with his foot. "You have a husband again."

"Well, it's about time," Alice said, turning over on her back and looking up at him, smiling in answer to his happy grin.

He stepped over her and went out on the diving board, leaping up and down on it, higher and higher each time, in smooth coordination, then went into a one and a half gainer, his body cutting into the water with a minimum of splash.

His head broke the surface. He looked up at his wife, and laughed in the sheer pleasure of being alive. A few swift strokes brought him to the foot of the ladder. He climbed, dripping water, to the dock, then sat down by his wife.

"Yep, it's done," he said. "How many days of our vacation left? Two? That's time enough for me to get a little tan. Might as well make the most of it. I'm going to be working harder this winter than I ever did in my life."

"But I thought you said your paper was done!"

"It is. But that's only the beginning. Instead of sending it in for publication, I'm going to submit it to the directors, with a request for facilities and personnel to conduct a line of research based on pages twenty-seven to thirty-two of the paper."

"And you think they'll grant your request?"

"There's no question about it," Dr. MacNare said, smiling confidently. "It's the most important line of research ever opened up to experimental psychology. They'll be forced to grant my request. It will put the university on the map!"

Alice laughed, and sat up and kissed him.

"Maybe they won't agree with you," she said. "Is it all right for me to read the paper?"

"I wish you would," he said. "Where's that son of mine? Upstream?" He leaped to his feet and went to the diving board again.

"Better walk along the bank, Joe. The stream is too swift."

"Nonsense!" Dr. MacNare said. He made a long shallow dive, then began swimming in a powerful crawl that took him upstream slowly. Alice stood on the dock watching him until he was lost to sight around the bend, then went into the cabin. The completed paper lay beside the typewriter.

ALICE HAD her doubts. "I'm not so sure the board will approve of this," she said. Dr. MacNare, somewhat exasperated, said, "What makes you think that? Pavlov experimented with his dog, physiological experiments with rats, rabbits, and other animals go on all the time. There's nothing cruel about it."

"Just the same..." Alice said. So Dr. MacNare cautiously resisted the impulse to talk about his paper with his fellow professors and his most intelligent students. Instead, he merely turned his paper into the board at the earliest opportunity and kept silent, waiting for their decision.

He hadn't long to wait. On the last Friday of September he received a note requesting his presence in the boardroom at three o'clock on Monday. He rushed home after his last class and told Alice about it.

"Let's hope their decision is favorable," she said.

"It has to be," Dr. MacNare answered with conviction.

He spent the weekend making plans. "They'll probably assign me a machinist and a couple of electronics experts from the hill," he told Alice. "I can use graduate students for work with the animals. I hope they give me Dr. Munitz from Psych as a consultant, because I like him much better than Veerhof. By early spring we should have things rolling."

Monday at three o'clock on the dot, Dr. MacNare knocked on the door of the boardroom, and entered. He was not unfamiliar with it, nor with the faces around the massive walnut conference table. Always before he had known what to expect—a brief commendation for the revisions in his textbook on calculus for its fifth printing, a nice speech from the president about his good work as a prelude to a salary raise—quiet, expected things. Nothing unanticipated had ever happened here.

Now, as he entered, he sensed a difference. All eyes were fixed on him, but not with admiration or friendliness. They were fixed more in the manner of a restaurateur watching the approach of a cockroach along the surface of the counter.

Suddenly the room seemed hot and stuffy. The confidence in Dr. MacNare's expression evaporated. He glanced back toward the door as though wishing to escape.

"So it's *you!*" the president said, setting the tone of what followed.

"This is *yours?*" the president added, picking up the neatly typed manuscript, glancing at it, and dropping it back on the table as though it were something unclean.

Dr. MacNare nodded, and cleared his throat nervously to say yes, but didn't get the chance.

"We—all of us—are amazed and shocked," the president said. "Of course, we understand that psychology is not your field, and you probably were thinking only from the mathematical viewpoint. We are agreed on that. What you propose, though..." He shook his head slowly. "It's not only out of the question, but I'm afraid I'm going to have to request that you forget the whole thing—put this paper where no one can see it, preferably destroy it. I'm sorry, Dr. MacNare, but the university simply cannot afford to be associated with such a thing even remotely. I'll put it bluntly because I feel strongly about it, as do the other members of the Board. *If this paper is published or in any way comes to light, we will be forced to request your resignation from the faculty.*"

"But why?" Dr. MacNare asked in complete bewilderment.

"Why?" another board member exploded, slapping the table. "It's the most inhuman thing I ever heard of, strapping a newborn animal onto some kind of frame and tying its legs to control levers, with the intention of never letting it free. The most fiendish and inhuman torture imaginable! If you didn't have such an outstanding record I would be for demanding your resignation at once."

"But that's not true!" Dr. MacNare said. "It's not torture! Not in any way! Didn't you read the paper? Didn't you understand that—"

"I read it," the man said. "We all read it. Every word."

"Then you should have understood—" Dr. MacNare said.

"We read it," the man repeated, "and we discussed some aspects of it with Dr. Veerhof without bringing your paper into it, nor your name."

"Oh," Dr. MacNare said. "Veerhof…"

"He says experiments, very careful experiments, have already been conducted along the lines of getting an animal to understand a symbol system and it can't be done. The nerve paths aren't there. Your line of research, besides being inhumanly cruel, would accomplish nothing."

"Oh," Dr. MacNare said, his eyes flashing. "So you know all about the results of an experiment in an untried field without performing the experiments!"

"According to Dr. Veerhof that field is not untried but rather well explored," the board member said. "Giving an animal the means to make vocal sounds would not enable it to form a symbol system."

"I disagree," Dr. MacNare said, seething. "My studies indicate clearly—"

"I think," the president said with a firmness that demanded the floor, "our position has been made very clear, Dr. MacNare. The matter is now closed. Permanently. I hope you will have the good sense, if I may use such a strong term, to forget the whole thing. For the good of your career and your very nice wife and son. That is all." He held the manuscript toward Dr. MacNare.

"I can't understand their attitude!" Dr. MacNare said to Alice when he told her about it.

"Possibly I can understand it a little better than you, Joe," Alice said thoughtfully. "I had a little of what I think they feel, when I first read your paper. A—a prejudice against the idea of it, is as closely as I can describe it. Like it would be violating the order of nature, giving an animal a soul, in a way."

"Then you feel as they do?" Dr. MacNare said.

"I didn't say that, Joe." Alice put her arms around her husband and kissed him fiercely. "Maybe I feel just the opposite, that if there is some way to give an animal a soul, we should do it."

Dr. MacNare chuckled. "It wouldn't be quite that cosmic. An animal can't be given something it doesn't have already. All that can be done is to give it the means to fully capitalize on what it has. Animals—man included—can only do by observing the results. When you move a finger, what you really do is send a neural impulse out from the brain along one particular nerve or one particular set of nerves, but you can never learn that, nor just what it is you do. All that you can know is that when you do a definite *something* your eyes and sense of touch bring you the information that your finger moved. But if that finger were attached to a voice element that made the sound *ah*, and you could never see your finger, all you could ever know is that when you did that particular *something* you made a certain vocal sound. Changing the resultant effect of mental commands to include things normally impossible to you may expand the potential of your mind, but it won't give you a soul if you don't have one to begin with."

"You're using Veerhof's arguments on me," Alice said. "And I think we're arguing from separate definitions of a soul. I'm afraid of it, Joe. It would be a tragedy, I think, to give some animal—a rat, maybe—the soul of a poet, and then have it discover that it is only a rat."

"Oh," Dr. MacNare said. "*That* kind of soul. No, I'm not that optimistic about the results. I think we'd be lucky to get any results at all, a limited vocabulary that the animal would use meaningfully. But I do think we'd get that."

"It would take a lot of time and patience."

"And we'd have to keep the whole thing secret from everyone," Dr. MacNare said. "We couldn't even let Paul have an inkling of it, because he might say something to one of his playmates, and it would get back to some member of the board. How could we keep it secret from Paul?"

"Paul knows he's not allowed in your study," Alice said. "We could keep everything there—and keep the door locked."

"Then it's settled?"

"Wasn't it, from the very beginning?" Alice put her arms around her husband and her cheek against his ear to hide her worried expression. "I love you, Joe. I'll help you in any way I can. And if we haven't enough in the savings account, there's always what Mother left me."

"I hope we won't have to use any of it, sweetheart," he said.

The following day Dr. MacNare was an hour and a half late coming home from the campus. He had been, he announced casually, to a pet store.

"We'll have to hurry," said Alice. "Paul will be home any minute."

She helped him carry the packages from the car to the study. Together they moved things around to make room for the gleaming new cages with their white rats and hamsters and guinea pigs. When it was done they stood arm in arm viewing their new possession.

TO ALICE MacNare, just the presence of the animals in her husband's study brought the research project into reality. As the days passed that romantic feeling became fact.

"We're going to have to do together," Joe MacNare told her at the end of the first week, "what a team of a dozen specialists in separate fields should be doing. Our first job, before we can do anything else, is to study the natural movements of each species and translate them into patterns of robot directives."

"Robot directives?"

"I visualize it this way," Dr. MacNare said. "The animal will be strapped comfortably in a frame so that its body can't move but its legs can. Its legs will be attached to four separate, free-moving levers which make a different electrical contact for every position. Each electrical contact, or control switch, will cause the robot body to do one specific thing, such as move a leg, utter some particular sound through its voice box, or move just one finger. Can you visualize that, Alice?"

Alice nodded.

"Okay. Now, one leg has to be used for nothing but voice sounds. That leaves three legs for control of the movements of the robot body. In body movement there will be simultaneous movements and sequences. A simple sequence can be controlled by one leg. All movements of the robot will have to be reduced to not more than three concurrent sequences of movement of the animal's legs. Our problem, then, is to make the unlearned and the most natural movements of the legs of the animal control the robot body's movements in a functional manner."

Endless hours were consumed in this initial study and mapping. Alice worked at it while her husband was at the university and Paul was at school. Dr. MacNare rushed home each day to go over what she had done and continue the work himself.

He grew more and more grudging of the time his classes took. In December he finally wrote to the three technical journals that had been expecting papers from him for publication during the year that he would be too busy to do them.

By January the initial phase of research was well enough along so that Dr. MacNare could begin planning the robot. For this he set up a workshop in the garage.

In early February he finished what he called the "test frame." After Paul had gone to bed, Dr. MacNare brought the test frame into the study from the garage. To Alice it looked very much like the insides of a radio.

She watched while he placed a husky-looking male white rat in the body harness fastened to the framework of aluminum and tied its legs to small metal rods.

Nothing happened except that the rat kept trying to get free, and the small metal rods tied to its feet kept moving in pivot sockets.

"Now!" Dr. MacNare said excitedly, flicking a small toggle switch on the side of the assembly.

Immediately a succession of vocal sounds erupted from the speaker. They followed one another, making no sensible word.

"*He's* doing that," Dr. MacNare said triumphantly.

"If we left him in that, do you think he'd eventually associate his movements with the sounds?"

"It's possible. But that would be more on the order of what we do when we drive a car. To some extent a car becomes an extension of the body, but you're always aware that your hands are on the steering wheel, your foot on the gas pedal or brake. You extend your awareness consciously. You interpret a slight tremble in the steering wheel as a shimmy in the front wheels. You're oriented primarily to your body and only secondarily to the car as an extension of you."

Alice closed her eyes for a moment. "Mm hmm," she said.

"And that's the best we could get, using a rat that knows already it's a rat."

Alice stared at the struggling rat, her eyes round with comprehension, while the loudspeaker in the test frame said, "Ag-pr-ds-raf-os-dg…"

Dr. MacNare shut off the sound and began freeing the rat.

"By starting with a newborn animal and never letting it know what it is," he said, "we can get a complete extension of the animal into the machine, in its orientation. So complete that if you took it out of the machine after it grew up, it would have no more idea of what had happened than—than your brain if it were taken out of your head and put on a table!"

"Now I'm getting that *feeling* again, Joe," Alice said, laughing nervously. "When you said that about my brain I thought, 'Or my soul?'"

Dr. MacNare put the rat back in its cage.

"There might be a valid analogy there," he said slowly. "If we have a soul that survives after death, what is it like? It probably interprets its surroundings in terms of its former orientation in the body."

"That's a little of what I mean," Alice said. "I can't help it, Joe. Sometimes I feel so sorry for whatever baby animal you'll eventually use that I want to cry. I feel so sorry for it, because *we will never dare let it know what it really is!*"

"That's true. Which brings up another line of research that should be the work of one expert on the team I ought to have for this. As it is, I'll turn it over to you to do while I build the robot."

"What's that?"

"Opiates," Dr. MacNare said. "What we want is an opiate that can be used on a small animal every few days, so that we can take it out of the robot, bathe it, and put it back again without its knowing about it. There probably is no ideal drug. We'll have to test the more promising ones."

Later that night, as they lay beside each other in the silence and darkness of their bedroom, Dr. MacNare sighed deeply.

"So many problems," he said. "I sometimes wonder if we can solve them all. *See* them all…"

To Alice MacNare, later, that night in early February marked the end of the first phase of research—the point where two alternative futures hung in the balance, and either could have been taken. That night she might have said, there in the darkness, "Let's drop it," and her husband might have agreed. She thought of saying it. She even opened her mouth to say it. But her husband's soft snores suddenly broke the silence of the night. The moment of return had passed.

MONTH followed month. To Alice it was a period of rushing from kitchen to hypodermic injections to vacuum cleaner to hypodermic injections, her key to the study in constant use.

Paul, nine years old now, took to spring baseball and developed an indifference to TV, much to the relief of both his parents.

In the garage workshop Dr. MacNare made parts for the robot, and kept a couple of innocent projects going which he worked on when his son Paul evinced his periodic curiosity about what was going on.

Spring became summer. For six weeks Paul went to Scout camp, and during those six weeks Dr. MacNare reorganized the entire research project in line with what it would be in the fall. A decision was made to use only white rats from then on. The rest of the animals were sold to a pet store, and a system for automatically feeding, watering, and keeping the cages clean was installed in preparation for a much needed two weeks vacation at the cabin.

When the time came to go, they had to tear themselves away from their work by an effort of will—aided by the realization that they could get little done with Paul underfoot.

September came all too soon. By mid-September both Dr. MacNare and his wife felt they were on the home stretch. Parts of the robot were going together and being tested, the female white rats were being bred at the rate of one a week so that when the robot was completed there would be a supply of newborn rats on hand.

October came, and passed. The robot was finished, but there were minor defects in it that had to be corrected.

"Adam," Dr. MacNare said one day, "will have to wear this robot all his life. It has to be just right."

And with each litter of baby rats Alice said. "I wonder which one is Adam."

They talked of Adam often now, speculating on what he would be like. It was almost, they decided, as though Adam were their second child.

And finally, on November 2, 1956, everything was ready. Adam would be born in the next litter due in about three days.

The amount of work that had gone into preparation for the great moment is beyond conception. Four file cabinet drawers were filled with notes. By actual measurement seventeen feet of shelf space was filled with books on the thousand and one subjects that had to be mastered. The robot itself was a masterpiece of engineering that would have done credit to the research staff of a watch manufacturer. The vernier adjustments alone, used to compensate daily for the rat's growth, had eight patentable features.

And the skills that had had to be acquired! Alice, who had never before had a hypodermic syringe in her hand, could now inject a precisely measured amount of opiate into the tiny body of a baby rat with calm confidence in her skill.

After such monumental preparation, the great moment itself was anticlimactic. While the mother of Adam was still preoccupied with the birth of the remainder of the brood, Adam, a pink helpless thing about the size of a little finger, was picked up and transferred to the head of the robot.

His tiny feet, which he would never know existed, were fastened with gentle care to the four control rods. His tiny head was thrust into a helmet attached to a pivot-mounted optical system, ending in the lenses that served the robot for eyes. And finally a transparent plastic cover contoured to the shape of the back of a human head was fastened in place. Through it his feeble attempts at movement could be easily observed.

Thus, Dr. MacNare's Adam was born into his body, and the time of the completion of his birth was one-thirty in the afternoon on the fifth day of November, 1956.

In the ensuing half-hour all the cages of rats were removed from the study, the floor was scrubbed, and deodorizers were sprayed, so that no slightest trace of Adam's lowly origins remained. When this was done, Dr. MacNare loaded the cages into his car and drove them to a pet store that had agreed to take them.

When he returned, he joined Alice in the study, and at five minutes before four, with Alice hovering anxiously beside him, he opened the cover on Adam's chest and turned on the master switch that gave Adam complete dominion over his robot body.

Adam was beautiful—and monstrous. Made of metal from the neck down, but shaped to be covered by padding and skin in human semblance. From the neck up the job was done. The face was human, masculine, handsome, much like that of a clothing store dummy except for its mobility of expression, and the incongruity of the rest of the body.

The voice-control lever and contacts had been designed so that the ability to produce most sounds would have to be discovered by Adam as he gained control of his natural right front leg. Now the only sounds being uttered were *oh, ah, mm,* and *ll,* in random order. Similarly, the only movements of his arms and legs were feeble, like those of a human baby. The tremendous strength in his limbs was something he would be unable to tap fully until he had learned conscious coordination.

After a while Adam became silent and without movement. Alarmed, Dr. MacNare opened the instrument panel in the abdomen. The instruments showed that Adam's pulse and respiration were normal. He had fallen asleep.

Dr. MacNare and his wife stole softly from the study, and locked the door.

AFTER A FEW days, with the care and feeding of Adam all that remained of the giant research project, the pace of the days shifted to that of long-range patience.

"It's just like having a baby," Alice said.

"You know something?" Dr. MacNare asked. "I've had to resist passing out cigars. I hate to say it, but I'm prouder of Adam than I was of Paul when he was born."

"So am I, Joe," Alice said quietly. "But I'm getting a little of that scared feeling back again."

"In what way?"

"He watches me. Oh, I know it's natural for him to, but I do wish you had made the eyes so that his own didn't show as little dark dots in the center of the iris."

"It couldn't be helped," Dr. MacNare said. "He has to be able to see, and I had to set up the system of mirrors so that the two axes of vision would be three inches apart as they are in the average human pair of eyes."

"Oh, I know," said Alice. "Probably it's just something I've seized on. But when he watches me, I find myself holding my breath in fear that he can read in my expression the secret we have to keep from him, that he is a rat."

"Forget it, Alice. That's outside his experience and beyond his comprehension."

"I know," Alice sighed. "When he begins to show some of the signs of intelligence a baby has, I'll be able to think of him as a human being."

"Sure, darling," Dr. MacNare said;

"Do you think he ever will?"

"That," Dr. MacNare said, "is the big question. I think he will. I think so now even more than I did at the start. Aside from eating and sleeping, he has no avenue of expression except his robot body, and *no source of reward except that of making sense— human sense.*"

The days passed, and became weeks, then months. During the daytime when her husband was at the university and her son was at school, Alice would spend most of her hours with Adam, forcing herself to smile at him and talk to him as she had to Paul when he was a baby. But when she watched his motions through the transparent back of his head, his leg motions remained those of attempted walking and attempted running.

Then one day when Adam was four months old, things changed—as abruptly as the turning on of a light.

The unrewarding walking and running movements of Adam's little legs ceased. It was evening, and both Dr. MacNare and his wife were there.

For a few seconds there was no sound or movement from the robot body. Then, quite deliberately, Adam said, "Ah."

"Ah," Dr. MacNare echoed. "Mm. Mm, ah. Ma-ma."

"Mm," Adam said.

The silence in the study became absolute. The seconds stretched into eternities. Then—

"Mm, ah," Adam said. "Mm, ah."

Alice began crying with happiness.

"Mm, ah," Adam said. "Mm, ah. Ma-ma. Mamamamama."

Then, as though the effort had been too much for Adam, he went to sleep.

Having achieved the impossible, Adam seemed to lose interest in it. For two days he uttered nothing more than an occasional involuntary syllable.

"I would call that as much of an achievement as speech itself," Dr. MacNare said to his wife. "His right front leg has asserted its independence. If each of his other three legs can do as well, he can control the robot body."

It became obvious that Adam was trying. Though the movements of his body remained non-purposive, the pauses in those movements became more and more pregnant with what was obviously mental effort.

During that period there was of course room for argument and speculation about it, and even a certain amount of humor. Had Adam's right front leg, at the moment of achieving meaningful speech suffered a nervous breakdown? What would a psychiatrist have to say about a white rat that had a nervous breakdown in its right front leg?

"The worst part about it," Dr. MacNare said to his wife, "is that if he fails to make it he'll have to be killed. He can't have permanent frustration forced onto him, and, by now, returning him to his natural state would be even worse."

"And he has such a stout little heart," Alice said. "Sometimes when he looks at me I'm sure he knows what is happening and he wants me to know he's trying."

When they went to bed that night they were more discouraged than they had ever been.

Eventually the slept. When the alarm went off, Alice slipped into her robe and went into the study first, as she always did.

A moment later she was back in the bedroom, shaking her husband's shoulder.

"Joe!" she whispered. "Wake up! Come into the study!"

He leaped out of bed and rushed past her. She caught up with him and pulled him to a stop.

"Take it easy, Joe," she said. "Don't alarm him."

"Oh." Dr. MacNare relaxed. "I thought something had happened."

"Something has!"

They stopped in the doorway of the study. Dr. MacNare sucked in his breath sharply, but remained silent.

Adam seemed oblivious of their presence. He was too interested in something else.

He was interested in his hands. He was holding his hands up where he could see them, and he was moving them independently, clenching and unclenching the metal fingers with slow deliberation.

Suddenly the movement stopped. He had become aware of them. Then, impossibly, unbelievably, he spoke.

"Mama," Adam said. Then, "Papa."

"Adam!" Alice sobbed, rushing across the study to him and sinking down beside him. Her arms went around his metal body. "Oh, Adam," she cried happily.

IT WAS the beginning. The date of that beginning is not known. Alice MacNare believes it was early in May, but more probably it was in April. There was no time to keep notes. In fact, there was no longer a research project nor any thought of one. Instead, there was Adam, the person. At least, to Alice he became that, completely. Perhaps, also, to Dr. MacNare.

Dr. MacNare quite often stood behind Adam where he could watch the rat body through the transparent skull case while Alice engaged Adam's attention. Alice did the same, at times, but she finally refused to do so any more. The sight of Adam the rat, his body held in a net attached to the frame, his head covered by the helmet, his four legs moving independently of one another with little semblance of walking or running motion nor even of coordination, but with swift darting motions and pauses pregnant with meaning, brought back to Alice the old feeling of vague fear, and a tremendous surge of pity for Adam that made her want to cry.

Slowly, subtly, Adam's rat body became to Alice a pure brain, and his legs four nerve ganglia. A brain covered with short white fur; and when she took him out of his harness under opiate to bathe him, she bathed him as gently and carefully as any brain surgeon sponging a cortical surface.

Once started, Adam's mental development progressed rapidly. Dr. MacNare began making notes again on June 2, 1957, just ten days before the end, and it is to these notes that we go for an insight into Adam's mind.

On June 4th Dr. MacNare wrote, "I am of the opinion that Adam will never develop beyond the level of a moron, in the scale of human standards. He would probably make a good factory worker or chauffeur, in a year or two. But he is consciously aware of himself as Adam, he thinks in words and simple sentences with an accurate understanding of their meaning, and he is able to do new things from spoken instructions. There is no question, therefore, but that he has an integrated mind, entirely human in every respect."

On June 7th Dr. MacNare wrote, "Something is developing which I hesitate to put down on paper—for a variety of reasons. Creating Adam was a scientific experiment, nothing more than that. Both the premises on which the project was based have been proven: that the principle of verification is the main factor in learned response, and that, given the proper conditions, some animals are capable of abstract symbol systems and therefore of thinking with words to form meaningful concepts.

"Nothing more was contemplated in the experiment. I stress this because—Adam is becoming deeply religious—and before any mistaken conclusions are drawn from this I will explain what caused this development. It was an oversight of a type that is bound to happen in any complex project.

"Alice's experimental data on the effects of opiates, and especially the data on increasing the dose to offset growing tolerance, were based on observation of the subject alone, without any knowledge of the mental aspects of increased tolerance—which would of course be impossible except with human subjects.

"Unknown to us, Adam has been becoming partly conscious during his bath. Just conscious enough to be vaguely aware of certain sensations, and to remember them afterward. Few, if any, of these half remembered sensations are such that he can fit them into the pattern of his waking reality.

"The one that has had the most pronounced influence on him is, to quote him, 'Feel clean inside. Feel good.' Quite obviously this sensation is caused by his bath.

"With it is a distinct feeling of disembodiment, of being— and these are his own words—'outside my body'! This, of course, is an accurate realization, because to him the robot is his body, and he knows nothing of the existence of his actual, living, rat body.

"In addition to these two effects, there is a third one. A feeling of walking, and sometimes of floating, of stumbling over things he can't see, of talking, of being talked to by disembodied voices.

"The explanation of this is also obvious. When he is being bathed his legs are moved about. Any movement of a leg is to him either a spoken sound or a movement of some part of his robot body. Any movement of his right front leg, for example, tells his mind that he is making a sound. But, since his leg is not connected to the sound system of his robot body, his ears bring no physical verification of the sound. The mental anticipation of that verification then becomes a disembodied voice to him.

"The end result of all this is that Adam is becoming convinced that there is a hidden side of things (which there is), and that it is supernatural (which it is, *in the framework of his orientation*).

"What we are going to have to do is make sure he is completely unconscious before taking him out and bathing him. His mental health is far more important than exploring the interesting avenues opened up by this unforeseen development.

"I do intend, however, to make one simple test, while he is fully awake, before dropping this avenue of investigation."

Dr. MacNare does not state in his notes what this test was to be; but his wife says that it probably refers to the time when he pinched Adam's tail and Adam complained of a sudden, violent headache. This transference is the one well known to doctors. Unoriented pain in the human body manifests itself as a "headache," when the source of the pain is actually the stomach, or the liver, or anyone of a hundred spots in the body.

The last notes made by Dr. MacNare were those of June 11, 1957, and are unimportant except for the date. We return, therefore, to actual events, so far as they can be reconstructed.

We have said little or nothing about Dr. MacNare's life at the university after embarking on the research project, nor of the social life of the MacNares. As conspirators, they had kept up their social life to avoid any possibility of the board getting curious about any radical change in Dr. MacNare's habits; but as time went on both Dr. MacNare and his wife became so engrossed in their project that only with the greatest reluctance did they go anywhere.

The annual faculty party at Professor Long's on June 12th was something they could not evade. Not to have gone would have been almost tantamount to a resignation from the university.

"Besides," Alice had said when they discussed the matter in May, "isn't it about time to do a little hinting that you have something up your sleeve?"

"I don't know, Alice," Dr. MacNare had said. Then a smile quirked his lips and he said, "I wouldn't mind telling off Veerhof. I've never gotten over his deciding something was impossible without enough data to pass judgment." He frowned. "We are going to have to let the world know about Adam pretty soon, aren't we? That's something I haven't thought about. But not yet. Next fall will be time enough."

"DON'T forget, Joe," Alice said at dinner. "Tonight's the party at Professor Long's."

"How can I forget with you reminding me?" Dr. MacNare said, winking at his son.

"And you, Paul," Alice said. "I don't want you leaving the house. You understand? You can watch TV, and I want you in bed by nine thirty."

"Ah, Mom!" Paul protested. "Nine thirty?" He suppressed a grin. He had a party of his own planned.

"And you can wipe the dishes for me. We have to be at Professor Long's by eight o'clock."

"I'll help you," Dr. MacNare said.

"No, you have to get ready. Besides, don't you have to look up something for one of the faculty?"

"I'd forgotten," said Dr. MacNare. "Thanks for reminding me."

After dinner he went directly to the study. Adam was sitting on the floor playing with his wooden blocks. They were alphabet blocks, but he didn't know that yet. The summer project was going to be teaching him the alphabet. Already, though, he preferred placing them in straight rows rather than stacking them up.

At seven o'clock Alice rapped on the door to the study.

"Time to get dressed, Joe," she called.

"You'll be all right while we're gone, Adam?" Dr. MacNare said.

"I be all right, papa," Adam said. "I sleep."

"That's good," Dr. MacNare said. "I'll turn out the light."

At the door he waited until Adam had sat down in the chair he always slept on, and settled himself. Then he pushed the switch just to the right of the door and went out.

"Hurry, dear," Alice called. "I'm hurrying," Dr. MacNare protested—and, for the first time, he forgot to lock the study door.

The bathroom was next to the study, the wall between them soundproofed by a ceiling-high bookshelf in the study filled with thousands of books. On the other side was the master bedroom, with a closet with sliding panels that opened both on the bedroom and the bathroom. These sliding panels were partly open, so that Dr. MacNare and Alice could talk.

"Did you lock the study door?"

"Of course," Dr. MacNare said. "But I'll check before we leave."

"How is Adam taking being alone tonight?" Alice called.

"Okay," Dr. MacNare said. "Damn!"

"What's the matter, Joe?"

"I forgot to get razor blades."

The conversation died down.

Alice MacNare finished dressing.

"Aren't you ready yet, Joe?" she called. "It's almost a quarter to eight."

"Be right with you. I nicked myself shaving with an old blade. The bleeding's almost stopped now."

Alice went into the living room. Paul had turned on the TV and was sprawled out on the rug.

"You be sure and stay home, and be in bed by nine thirty, Paul," she said. "Promise?"

"Ah, Mom," he protested. "Well, all right."

Dr. MacNare came into the room, still working on his tie. A moment later they went out the front door. They had been gone less than five minutes when there was a knock. Paul jumped to his feet and opened the door.

"Hi, Fred, Tony, Bill," he said.

The boys, all nine years old, sprawled on the rug and watched television. It became eight o'clock, eight-thirty, and finally five minutes to nine. The commercial began.

"Where's your bathroom?" Tony asked.

"In there," Paul said, pointing vaguely at the doorway to the hall.

Tony got up off the floor and went into the hall. He saw several doors, all looking much alike. He picked one and opened it. It was dark inside. He felt along the wall for a light switch and found it. Light flooded the room. He stared at what he saw for perhaps ten seconds, then turned and ran down the hall to the living room.

"Say, Paul!" he said. "You never said anything about having a real honest to gosh robot!"

"What are you talking about?" Paul said.

"In that room in there!" Tony said. "Come on. I'll show you!"

The TV program forgotten, Paul, Fred, and Bill crowded after him. A moment later they stood in the doorway to the study, staring in awe at the strange figure of metal that sat motionless in a chair across the room.

Adam, it seems certain, was asleep, and had not been wakened by this intrusion nor the turning on of the light.

"Gee!" Paul said. "It belongs to Dad. We'd better get out of here."

"Naw," Tony said with a feeling of proprietorship at having been the original discoverer. "Let's take a look. He'll never know about it."

They crossed the room slowly, until they were close up to the robot figure, marveling at it, moving around it.

"Say!" Bill whispered, pointing. "What's that in there? It looks like a white rat with its head stuck into that kind of helmet thing."

They stared at it a moment.

"Maybe it's dead. Let's see."

"How you going to find out?"

"See those hinges on the cover?" Tony said importantly. "Watch." With cautious skill he opened the transparent back half of the dome, and reached in, wrapping his fingers around the white rat.

He was unable to get it loose, but he succeeded in pulling its head free of the helmet.

At the same time Adam awoke.

"Ouch!" Tony cried, jerking his hand away. "He bit me!"

"He's alive all right," Bill said. "Look at him glare!" He prodded the body of the rat and pulled his hand away quickly as the rat lunged.

"Gee, look at its eyes," Paul said nervously. "They're getting bloodshot."

"Dirty old rat!" Tony said vindictively, jabbing at the rat with his finger and evading the snapping teeth.

"Get its head back in there!" Paul said desperately. "I don't want papa to find out we were in here!" He reached in, driven by desperation, pressing the rat's head between his fingers and forcing it back into the tight fitting helmet.

Immediately screaming sounds erupted from the lips of the robot. (It was determined by later examination that only when the rat's body was completely where it should be were the circuits operable.)

"Let's get out of here!" Tony shouted, and dived for the door, thereby saving his life.

"Yeah! Let's get out of here!" Fred shouted as the robot figure rose to its feet. Terror enabled him to escape.

Bill and Paul delayed an instant too long. Metal fingers seized them. Bill's arm snapped halfway between shoulder and elbow. He screamed with pain and struggled to free himself.

Paul was unable to scream. Metal fingers gripped his shoulder, with a metal thumb thrust deeply against his larynx, paralyzing his vocal cords.

Fred and Tony had run into the front room. There they waited, ready to start running again. They could hear Bill's screams. They could hear a male voice jabbering nonsense, and finally repeating over and over again, "Oh my, oh my, oh my," in a tone all the more horrible because it portrayed no emotion whatever.

Then there was silence.

The silence lasted several minutes. Then Bill began to sniffle, rubbing his knuckles in his eyes. "I wanta go home," he whimpered.

"Me too."

They took each other's hand and tiptoed to the front door, watching the open doorway to the hall. When they reached the front door Tony opened it, and when it was open they ran, not stopping to close the door behind them.

THERE ISN'T much more to tell. It is known that Tony and Bill arrived at their respective homes, saying nothing of what had happened. Only later did they come forward and admit their share in the night's events.

Joe and Alice MacNare arrived home from the party at Professor Long's at twelve thirty, finding the front door wide open, the lights on in the living room, and the television on.

Sensing that something was wrong, Alice hurried to her son's room and discovered he wasn't there. While she was doing that, Joe shut the front door and turned off the television.

Alice returned to the living room, eyes round with alarm, and said, "Paul's not in his room!"

"Adam!" Joe croaked, and rushed into the hallway, with Alice following more slowly.

She reached the open door of the study in time to see the robot figure pounce on Joe and fasten its metal fingers about his throat, crushing vertebrae and flesh alike.

Oblivious to her own danger, she rushed to rescue her already dead husband, but the metal fingers were inflexible. Belatedly she abandoned the attempt and ran into the hallway to the phone.

When the police arrived, they found her slumped against the wall in the hallway. She pointed toward the open doorway of the study, without speaking.

The police rushed into the study. At once there came the sounds of shots. Dozens of them, it seemed. Later both policemen admitted that they lost their heads and fired until their guns were empty.

But it was not yet the end of Adam.

It would perhaps be impossible to conceive the full horror of his last hours, but we can at least make a guess. Asleep when the boys entered the study, he awakened to a world he had never before perceived except very vaguely and under the soporific veil of opiate.

But it was a world vastly different even than that. There is no way of knowing what he saw—probably blurred ghostly figures, monstrous beyond the ability of his mind to grasp, for his eyes were adjusted only to the series of prisms and lenses that enabled him to see and coordinate the images brought to him through the eyes of the robot.

He saw these impossible figures, he felt pain and torture that were not of the flesh as he knew it, but of the spirit; agony beyond agony administered by what he could only believe were fiends from some nether hell.

And then, abruptly, as ten-year-old Paul shoved his head back into the helmet, the world he had come to believe was reality returned. It was as though he had returned to the body from some awful pit of hell, with the soul sickness still with him.

Before him he saw four humanlike figures of reality, but beings unlike the only two he had ever seen. Smaller, seeming to be a part of the unbelievable nightmare he had been in. Two of them fled, two were within his grasp.

Perhaps he didn't know what he was doing when he killed Paul and Bill. It's doubtful if he had the ability to think at all then, only to tremble and struggle in his pitiful little rat body, with the automatic mechanisms of the robot acting from those frantic motions.

But it is known that there were three hours between the deaths of the two boys and the entry of Dr. MacNare at twelve thirty, and during those three hours he would have had a chance to recover, and to think, and to partially rationalize the nightmare he had experienced in realms outside what to him was the world of reality.

Adam must certainly have been calm enough, rational enough, to recognize Dr. MacNare when he entered the study at twelve thirty.

Then why did Adam deliberately kill Joe by breaking his neck? Was it because, in that three hours, he had put together the evidence of his senses and come to the realization that he was not a man but a rat?

It's not likely. It is much more likely that Adam came to some aberrated conclusion dictated by the superstitious feelings that had grown so strongly into his strange and unique existence that dictated he must kill Joseph.

For it would have been impossible for him to have realized that he was only a rat. You see, Joseph MacNare had taken great care that Adam never, in all his life, should see *another* rat.

There remains only the end of Adam to relate.

Physically it can be only anticlimactic. With his metal body out of commission from a dozen or so shots, two of which destroyed the robot extensions of his eyes, he remained helpless until the coroner carefully removed him.

To the coroner he was just a white rat, and a strangely helpless one, unable to walk or stand as rats are supposed to. Also a strangely vicious one, with red little beads of eyes and lips drawn back from sharp teeth the same as some rabid wild animal.

The coroner had no way of knowing that somewhere in that small, menacing form there was a noble but lost mentality that knew itself as Adam, and held thoughts of a strange and wonderful realm of peace and splendor beyond the grasp of the normal physical senses.

The coroner could not know that the erratic motions of that small left front foot, if connected to the proper mechanisms, would have been audible as, perhaps, a prayer, a desperate plea to whatever lay in the Great Beyond to come down and rescue its humble creature.

"Vicious little bastard," the coroner said nervously to the homicide men gathered around Dr. MacNare's desk.

"Let me take care of it," said one of the detectives.

"No," the coroner answered. "I'll do it."

Quickly, so as not to be bitten, he picked Adam up by the tip of the tail and slammed him forcefully against the top of the desk.

THE END

King of the Hill

By JAMES BLISH

A madman can be prevented from bomb throwing—but a mad world?

IT DID COL. Hal Gascoigne no good whatsoever to know that he was the only man aboard Satellite Vehicle I. No good at all. He had stopped reminding himself of the fact some time back.

And now, as he sat sweating in the perfectly balanced air in front of the bombardier board, one of the men spoke to him again:

"Colonel, sir—"

Gascoigne swung around in the seat, and the sergeant— Gascoigne could almost remember the man's name—threw him a snappy Air Force salute.

"Well?"

"Bomb one is primed, sir. Your orders?"

"My orders?" Gascoigne said wonderingly. But the man was already gone. Gascoigne couldn't actually see the sergeant leave the control cabin, but he was no longer in it.

While he tried to remember, another voice rang in the cabin, as flat and razzy as all voices sound on an intercom.

"Radar room. On target."

A regular, meaningless peeping. The timing circuit had cut in.

Or had it? There was nobody in the radar room. There was nobody in the bomb hold, either. There had never been anybody on board SV-1 but Gascoigne, not since he had relieved Grinnell—and Grinnell had flown the station up here in the first place.

Then who had that sergeant been? His name was— It was—

The hammering of the teletype blanked it out. The noise was as loud as a pom-pom in the echoing metal cave. He got up and coasted across the deck to the machine, gliding in the gravity-free cabin with the ease of a man to whom free fall is almost second nature.

The teletype was silent by the time he reached it, and at first the tape looked blank. He wiped the sweat out of his eyes. There was the message.

MNBVCXZ LKJ HGFDS PYTR AOIU EUIO QPALZM

He got out his copy of "The Well-Tempered Pogo" and checked the speeches of Grundoon the Beaver-Chile for the key letter-sequence on which the code was based. There weren't very many choices. He had the clear in ten minutes.

BOMB ONE WASHINGTON 1700 HRS TAMMANANY

There it was. That was what he had been priming the bomb for. But there should have been earlier orders, giving him the go-ahead to prime. He began to rewind the paper.

It was all blank.

And—*Washington?* Why would the Joint Chiefs of Staff order him—

"Col. Gascoigne, sir—"

Gascoigne jerked around and returned the salute. "What's your name?" he snapped.

"Sweeney, sir," the Corporal said. Actually it didn't sound very much like Sweeney, or like anything else; it was just a noise. Yet the man's face looked familiar. "Ready with bomb two, sir."

The corporal saluted, turned, took two steps, and faded. He did not vanish, but he did not go out the door, either. He simply receded, became darker and harder to distinguish, and was no longer there. It was as though he and Gascoigne had disagreed about the effects of perspective in the glowing Earthlight, and Gascoigne had turned out to be wrong.

Numbly, he finished rewinding the paper. There was no doubt about it. There the order stood, black on yellow, as plain as plain. Bomb the capital of your own country at 1700 hours. Just incidentally, bomb your own home in the process, but don't give that a second thought. Be thorough, drop two bombs; don't worry about missing by a few seconds of arc and hitting Baltimore instead, or Silver Spring, or Milford, Del. CIG will give you the coordinates, but plaster the area anyhow. That's S.O.P.

With rubbery fingers, Gascoigne began to work the keys of the teletype. Sending on the frequency of Civilian Intelligence Group, he typed:

HELP SHOUT SERIOUS REPEAT SERIOUS PERSONNEL TROUBLE HERE STOP DON'T KNOW HOW LONG I CAN KEEP IT DOWN STOP URGENT GASCOIGNE SV ONE STOP

Behind him, the oscillator peeped rhythmically, timing the drive on the launching rack trunnion.

"Radar room. On target."

Gascoigne did not turn. He sat before the bombardier board and sweated in the perfectly balanced air. Inside his skull, his own voice was shouting:

STOP STOP STOP

THAT, as we reconstructed it afterwards, is how the SV-1 affair began. It was pure luck, I suppose, that Gascoigne sent his message direct to us. Civilian Intelligence Group is rarely called into an emergency when the emergency is just being born. Usually Washington tries to do the bailing job first. Then, when Washington discovers that the boat is still sinking, it passes the bailing can to us—usually with a demand that we transform it into a centrifugal pump, on the double.

We don't mind. Washington's failure to develop a government department similar in function to CIG is the reason why we're in business. The profits, of course, go to Affiliated Enterprises, Inc., the loose corporation of universities and industries, which put up the money to build ULTIMAC—and ULTIMAC is, in turn, the reason why Washington comes running to CIG so often.

This time, however, it did not look like the big computer was going to be of much use to us. I said as much to Joan Hadamard, our social sciences division chief, when I handed her the message.

"Um," she said. *'Personnel* trouble? What does he mean? He hasn't got any personnel, on that station."

This was no news to me. CIG provided the figures that got the SV-1 into its orbit in the first place, and it was on our advice that it carried only one man. The crew of a space vessel either has to be large or it has to be a lone man; there is no intermediate choice. And SV-1 wasn't big enough to carry a large crew—not to carry them and keep the men from flying at each other's throats sooner or later, that is.

"He means himself," I said. "That's why I don't think this is a job for the computer. It's going to have to be played person-to-person. It's my bet that the man's responsibility-happy; that danger was always implicit in the one-man recommendation."

"The only decent solution is a full complement," Joan agreed. "Once the Pentagon can get enough money from Congress to build a big station."

"What puzzles me is, why did he call us instead of his superiors?"

"That's easy. We process his figures. He trusts us. The Pentagon thinks we're infallible, and he's caught the disease from them."

"That's bad," I said.

"I've never denied it."

"No, what I mean is that it's bad that he called us instead of going through channels. It means that the emergency is at least as bad as he says it is."

I thought about it another precious moment longer while Joan did some quick dialing. As everybody on Earth—with the possible exception of a few Tibetans—already knew, the man who rode SV-1 rode with three hydrogen bombs immediately under his feet—bombs which he could drop with great precision on any spot on the Earth. Gascoigne was, in effect, the sum total of American foreign policy; he might as well have had "Spatial Supremacy" stamped on his forehead.

"What does the Air Force say?" I asked Joan as she hung up.

"They say they're a little worried about Gascoigne. He's a very stable man, but they had to let him run a month over his normal replacement time—why, they don't explain. He's been turning in badly garbled reports over the last week. They're thinking about giving him a dressing down."

"Thinking! They'd better be careful with that stuff, or they'll hurt themselves. Joan, somebody's going to have to go up there. I'll arrange fast transportation, and tell Gascoigne that help is coming. Who should go?"

"I don't have a recommendation," Joan said. "Better ask the computer."

I did so—on the double.

ULTIMAC said: *Harris.*

"Good luck, Peter," Joan said calmly. Too calmly.

"Yeah," I said. "Or good night."

EXACTLY WHAT I expected to happen as the ferry rocket approached SV-1, I don't now recall. I had decided that I couldn't carry a squad with me. If Gascoigne was really far-gone, he wouldn't allow a group of men to disembark; one man, on the other hand, he might pass. But I suppose I did expect him to put up an argument first.

Nothing happened. He did not challenge the ferry, and he didn't answer hails. Contact with the station was made through the radar automatics, and I was put off on board as routinely as though I was being let into a movie—but a lot more rapidly.

The control room was dark and confusing, and at first I didn't see Gascoigne anywhere. The Earthlight coming through the observation port was brilliant, but beyond the edges of its path the darkness was almost absolute, broken only by the little stars of indicator lenses.

A faint snicking sound turned my eyes in the right direction. There was Gascoigne. He was hunched over the bombardier board, his back to me. In one hand he held a small tool resembling a ticket-punch. Its jaws were nibbling steadily at a taut line of tape running between two spools; that had been the sound I'd heard. I recognized the device without any trouble; it was a programmer.

But why hadn't Gascoigne heard me come in? I hadn't tried to sneak up on him, there is no quiet way to come through an airlock anyway. But the punch went on snicking steadily.

"Col. Gascoigne," I said. There was no answer. I took a step forward. "Col. Gascoigne, I'm Harris of CIG. What are you doing?"

The additional step did the trick. "Stay away from me," Gascoigne growled, from somewhere way down in his chest. "I'm programming the bomb. Punching in the orders myself. Can't depend on my crew. Stay away."

"Give over for a minute. I want to talk to you."

"That's a new one," said Gascoigne, not moving. "Most of you guys were rushing to set up launchings before you even reported to me. Who the hell are you, anyhow? There's nobody on board, I know that well enough."

"I'm Peter Harris," I said. "From CIG—you called us, remember? You asked us to send help."

"Doesn't prove a thing. Tell me something I don't know. Then maybe I'll believe you exist. Otherwise—beat it."

"Nothing doing. Put down that punch."

Gascoigne straightened slowly and turned to look at me. "Well, you don't vanish, I'll give you that," he said. "What did you say your name was?"

"Harris. Here's my ID card."

Gascoigne took the plastic-coated card tentatively, and then removed his glasses and polished them. The gesture itself was perfectly ordinary, and wouldn't have surprised me—except that Gascoigne was not wearing glasses.

"It's hard to see in here," he complained. "Everything gets so steamed up. Hm. All right, you're real. What do you want?"

His finger touched a journal. Silently, the tape began to roll from one spool to another.

"Gascoigne, stop that thing. If you drop any bombs there'll be hell to pay. It's tense enough down below as it is. And there's no reason to bomb anybody."

"Plenty of reason," Gascoigne muttered. He turned toward the teletype, exposing to me for the first time a hip holster cradling a large, black automatic. I didn't doubt that he could draw it with fabulous rapidity, and put the bullets just where he wanted them to go. "I've got orders. There they are. See for yourself."

Cautiously, I sidled over to the teletype and looked. Except for Gascoigne's own message to CIG, and one from Joan Hadamard announcing that I was on my way, the paper was totally blank. There had been no other messages that day unless Gascoigne had changed the roll, and there was no reason why he should have. Those rolls last close to forever.

"When did this order come in?"

"This morning some time. I don't know. Sweeney!" he bawled suddenly, so loud that the paper tore in my hands. "When did that drop order come through?"

Nobody answered. But Gascoigne said almost at once, "There, you heard him."

"I didn't hear anything but you," I said, "and I'm going to stop that tape. Stand aside."

"Not a chance, Mister," Gascoigne said grimly. "The tape rides."

"Who's getting hit?"

"Washington," Gascoigne said, and passed his hand over his face. He appeared to have forgotten the imaginary spectacles.

"That's where your home is, isn't it?"

"It sure is," Gascoigne said. "It sure as hell is, Mister. Cute, isn't it?"

It was cute, all right. The Air Force boys at the Pentagon were going to be given about ten milliseconds to be sorry they'd refused to send a replacement for Gascoigne along with me.

*Replace him with who? We can't send his second alternate in anything
short of a week. The man has to have retraining, and the first alternate's in
the hospital with a ruptured spleen. Besides, Gascoigne's the best man for
the job; he's got to be bailed out somehow.*

Sure. With a psychological centrifugal pump, no doubt. In
the meantime the tape kept right on running.

"YOU MIGHT as well stop wiping your face, and turn down
the humidity instead," I said. "You've already smudged your
glasses again."

"Glasses?" Gascoigne muttered. He moved slowly across
the cabin, sailing upright like a sea horse, to the blank glass of a
closed port. I seriously doubted that he could see his reflection
in it, but maybe he didn't really want to see it. "I messed them
up, all right. Thanks." He went through the polishing routine
again.

A man who thinks he is wearing glasses also thinks he can't
see without them. I slid to the programmer and turned off the
tape. I was between the spools and Gascoigne now—but I
couldn't stay there forever.

"Let's talk a minute, Colonel," I said. "Surely it can't do any
harm."

Gascoigne smiled, with a sort of childish craft. "I'll talk," he
said. "Just as soon as you start that tape again. I was watching
you in the mirror, *before* I took my glasses off."

The liar. I hadn't made a move while he'd been looking into
that porthole. His poor pitiful weak old rheumy eyes had seen
every move I made while he was polishing his "glasses." I
shrugged and stepped away from the programmer.

"You start it," I said. "I won't take the responsibility."

"It's orders," Gascoigne said woodenly. He started the tape
running again. "It's their responsibility. What did you want to
talk to me about, anyhow?"

"Col. Gascoigne, have you ever killed anybody?"

He looked startled. "Yes, once I did," he said, almost
eagerly. "I crashed a plane into a house. Killed the whole

family. Walked away with nothing worse than a burned leg—good as new after a couple of muscle stabilizations. That's what made me shift from piloting to weapons; that leg's not quite good enough to fly with any more."

"Tough."

He snickered suddenly, explosively. "And now look at me," he said. "I'm going to kill my *own* family in a little while. And millions of other people. Maybe the whole world."

How long was "a little while"?

"What have you got against it?" I said.

"Against what—the world? Nothing. Not a damn thing. Look at me: I'm king of the hill up here. I can't complain."

He paused and licked his lips. "It was different when I was a kid," he said. "Not so dull, then. In those days you could get a real newspaper that you could unfold for the first time yourself, and pick out what you wanted to read. Not like now, when the news comes to you predigested on a piece of paper out of your radio. That's what's the matter with it, if you ask me."

"What's the matter with what?"

"With the news—that's why it's always bad these days. Everything's had something done to it. The milk is homogenized, the bread is sliced, the cars steer themselves, the phonographs will produce sounds no musical instrument could make. Too much meddling, too many people who can't keep their hands off things. Ever fire a kiln?"

"Me?" I said, startled.

"No, I didn't think so. Nobody makes pottery these days. Not by hand. And if they did, who'd buy it? They don't want something that's been made. They want something that's been Done To."

The tape kept on traveling. Down below, there was a heavy rumble, difficult to identify specifically: something heavy being shifted on tracks, or maybe a freight lock opening.

"So now you're going to Do Something to the Earth," I said slowly.

"Not me. It's orders."

"Orders from inside, Col. Gascoigne. There's nothing on the spools." What else could I do? I didn't have time to take him through two years of psychoanalysis and bring him to his own insight. Besides, I'm not licensed to practice medicine— not on Earth. "I didn't want to say so, but I have to now."

"Say what?" Gascoigne said suspiciously. "That I'm crazy or something?"

"No. I didn't say that. You did," I pointed out. "But I will tell you that that stuff about not liking the world these days is baloney. Or rationalization, if you want a nicer word. You're carrying a screaming load of guilt, Colonel, whether you're aware of it or not."

"I don't know what you're talking about. Why don't you just beat it?"

"No. And you know well enough. You fell all over yourself to tell me about the family you killed in your flying accident." I gave him ten seconds of silence, and then shot the question at him as hard as I could. *What was their name?*

"How do I know? Sweeney or something. Anything. I don't remember."

"Sure you do. Do you think that killing your own family is going to bring the Sweeney's back to life?"

Gascoigne's mouth twisted, but he seemed to be entirely unaware of the grimace. "That's all hogwash," he said. "I never did hold with that psychological claptrap. It's you that's handing out the baloney, not me."

"Then why are you being so vituperative about it? Hogwash, claptrap, baloney—you are working awfully hard to knock it down, for a man who doesn't believe in it."

"Go away," he said sullenly. "I've got my orders. I'm obeying them."

Stalemate. But there was no such thing as stalemate up here. Defeat was the word.

THE TAPE traveled. I did not know what to do. The last bomb problem CIG had tackled had been one we had set up ourselves; we had arranged for a dud to be dropped in New York harbor, to test our own facilities for speed in determining the nature of the missile. The situation on board SV-1 was completely different—

Whoa. Was it? Maybe I'd hit something there.

"Col. Gascoigne," I said slowly, "you might as well know now that it isn't going to work. Not even if you do get that bomb off."

"Yes, I can. What's to stop me?" He hooked one thumb in his belt, just above the holster, so that his fingertips rested on the breech of the automatic.

"Your bombs. They aren't alive."

Gascoigne laughed harshly and waved at the controls. "Tell that to the counter in the bomb hold. Go ahead. There's a meter you can read, right there on the bombardier board."

"Sure," I said. "The bombs are radioactive, all right. Have you ever checked their half-life?"

It was a long shot. Gascoigne was a weapons man; if it were possible to check half-life on board the SV-1, he would have checked it. But I didn't think it was possible.

"What would I do that for?"

"You wouldn't, being a loyal airman. You believe what your superiors tell you. But I'm a civilian, Colonel. There's no element in those bombs that will either fuse or fission. The half-life is too long for tritium or for lithium^6, and it's too short for uranium^{235} or radio-thorium. The stuff is probably strontium^{90}—in short, nothing but a bluff."

"By the time I finished checking that," Gascoigne said, "the bomb would be launched anyhow. And you haven't checked it, either. Try another tack."

"I don't need to. You don't have to believe me. We'll just sit here and wait for the bomb drop, and then the point will prove itself. After that, of course, you'll be court-martialed for firing a wild shot without orders. But since you're prepared to wipe out your own family, you won't mind a little thing like twenty years in the guardhouse."

Gascoigne looked at the silently rolling tape. "Sure," he said. "I've got the orders anyhow. The same thing would happen if I didn't obey them. If nobody gets hurt, so much the better."

A sudden spasm of emotion—I took it to be grief, but I could have been wrong—shook his whole frame for a moment. Again, he did not seem to notice it. I said: "That's right. Not even your family. Of course the whole world will know the station's a bluff, but if those are the orders—"

"I don't know," Gascoigne said harshly. "I don't know whether I even got any orders. I don't remember where I put them. Maybe they're not real." He looked at me confusedly, and his expression was frighteningly like that of a small boy making a confession.

"You know something?" he said. "I don't know what's real any more. I haven't been able to tell, ever since yesterday. I don't even know if you are real, or your ID card either. What do you think of that?"

"Nothing," I said.

"Nothing? Nothing! That's my trouble. Nothing! I can't tell what's nothing and what's something. You say the bombs are duds. All right. But what if *you're* the dud, and the bombs are real? Answer me that!"

His expression was almost triumphant now.

"The bombs are duds," I said. "And you've gone and steamed up your glasses again. Why don't you turn down the humidity, so you can see for three minutes hand running?"

Gascoigne leaned far forward, so far that he was perilously close to toppling, and peered directly into my face.

"Don't give me that," he said hoarsely. "Don't—give—me that—stuff."

I froze right where I was. Gascoigne watched my eyes for a while. Then, slowly, he put his hand on his forehead and began to wipe it downward. He smeared it over his face, in slow motion, all the way down to his chin.

Then he took the hand away and looked at it, as though it had just strangled him and he couldn't understand why. And finally he spoke.

"It—isn't true," he said dully. "I'm not wearing any glasses. Haven't worn glasses since I was ten. Not since I broke my last pair—playing King of the Hill."

He sat down before the bombardier board and put his head in his hands.

"You win," he said hoarsely. "I must be crazy as a loon. I don't know what I'm seeing and what I'm not. You better take this gun away. If I fired it I might even hit something."

"You're all right," I said. And I meant it; but I didn't waste any time all the same. The automatic first; then the tape. In that order, the sequence couldn't be reversed afterwards.

But the sound of the programmer's journal clicking to "Off" was as loud in that cabin as any gunshot.

"HE'LL BE all right," I told Joan afterwards. "He pulled himself through. I wouldn't have dared to throw it at any other man that fast—but he's got guts."

"Just the same," Joan said, "they'd better start rotating the station captains faster. The next man may not be so tough—and what if *he's* a sleepwalker?"

I didn't say anything. I'd had my share of worries for that week.

"You did a whale of a job yourself, Peter," Joan said. "I just wish we could bank it in the machine. We might need the data later."

"Well, why can't we?"

"The Joint Chiefs of Staff say no. They don't say why. But they don't want any part of it recorded in ULTIMAC—or anywhere else."

I stared at her. At first it didn't seem to make sense. And then it did—and that was worse.

"Wait a minute," I said. "Joan—does that mean what I think it means? Is 'Spatial Supremacy' just as bankrupt as 'Massive

Retaliation' was?   Is it possible that the satellite—and the bombs...   Is it possible that I was telling Gascoigne the truth about the bombs being duds?"

Joan shrugged.

"He that darkeneth counsel without wisdom," she said, "isn't earning his salary."

THE END

The Marching Morons

By C. M. KORNBLUTH

In the country of the blind, the one-eyed man, of course, is king. But how about a live-wire, smart businessman, in a civilization of 100% pure chumps?

SOME things had not changed. A potter's wheel was still a potter's wheel and clay was still clay. Efim Hawkins had built his shop near Goose Lake, which had a narrow band of good fat clay and a narrow beach of white sand. He fired three bottle-nosed kilns with willow charcoal from the wood lot. The wood lot was also useful for long walks while the kilns were cooling; if he let himself stay within sight of them, he would open them prematurely, impatient to see how some new shape or glaze had come through the fire and—*ping!*—the new shape or glaze would be good for nothing but the shard pile back of his slip tanks.

A business conference was in full swing in his shop, a modest cube of brick, tile-roofed, as the Chicago-Los Angeles "rocket" thundered overhead—very noisy, very swept-back, very fiery jets, shaped as sleekly swift-looking as an airborne barracuda.

The buyer from Marshall Fields was turning over a black-glazed one-liter carafe, nodding approval with his massive, handsome head. "This is real pretty," he told Hawkins and his own secretary, Gomez-Laplace. "This has got lots of what ya call real est'etic principles. Yeah, it is real pretty."

"How much?" the secretary asked the potter.

"Seven-fifty each in dozen lots," said Hawkins. "I ran up fifteen dozen last month."

"They are real est'etic," repeated the buyer from Fields. "I will take them all."

"I don't think we can do that, doctor," said the secretary. "They'd cost us $1,350. That would leave only $532 in our quarter's budget. And we still have to run down to East Liverpool to pick up some cheap dinner sets."

"Dinner sets?" asked the buyer, his big face full of wonder.

"Dinner sets. The department's been out of them for two months now. Mr. Garvy-Seabright got pretty nasty about it yesterday. Remember?"

"Garvy-Seabright, that meat-headed bluenose," the buyer said contemptuously. "He don't know nothin' about est'etics. Why for don't he lemme run my own department?" His eye fell on a stray copy of *Whambozambo Comix* and he sat down with it. An occasional deep chuckle or grunt of surprise escaped him as he turned the pages.

Uninterrupted, the potter and the buyer's secretary quickly closed a deal for two dozen of the liter carafes, "I wish we could take more," said the secretary, "but you heard what I told him. We've had to turn away customers for ordinary dinnerware because he shot the last quarter's budget on some Mexican piggy banks some equally enthusiastic importer stuck him with. The fifth floor is packed solid with them."

"I'll bet they look mighty est'etic."

"They're painted with purple cacti."

THE potter shuddered and caressed the glaze of the sample carafe.

The buyer looked up and rumbled, "Ain't you dummies through yakkin' yet? What good's a seckertary for if'n he don't take the burden of *de*-tail off'n my back, harh?"

"We're all through, doctor. Are you ready to go?"

The buyer grunted peevishly, dropped *Whambozambo Comix* on the floor and led the way out of the building and down the log corduroy road to the highway. His car was waiting on the concrete. It was, like all contemporary cars, too low-slung to get over the logs. He climbed down into the car and started the motor with a tremendous sparkle and roar.

"Gomez-Laplace," called out the potter under cover of the noise, "did anything come of the radiation program they were working on the last time I was on duty at the Pole?"

"The same old fallacy," said the secretary gloomily. "It stopped us on mutation, it stopped us on culling, it stopped us on segregation, and now it's stopped us on hypnosis."

"Well, I'm scheduled back to the grind in nine days. Time for another firing right now. I've got a new luster to try..."

"I'll miss you. I shall be 'vacationing'—running the drafting room of the New Century Engineering Corporation in Denver. They're going to put up a two hundred-story office building, and naturally somebody's got to be on hand."

"Naturally," said Hawkins with a sour smile.

There was an ear-piercingly-sweet blast as the buyer leaned on the horn button. Also, a yard-tall jet of what looked like flame spurted up from the car's radiator cap; the car's power plant was a gas turbine, and had no radiator.

"I'm coming, doctor," said the secretary dispiritedly. He climbed down into the car and it whooshed off with much flame and noise.

The potter, depressed, wandered back up the corduroy road and contemplated his cooling kilns. The rustling wind in the boughs was obscuring the creak and mutter of the shrinking refractory brick. Hawkins wondered about the number two kiln—a reduction fire on a load of lusterware mugs. Had the clay chinking excluded the air? Had it been a properly smoky blaze? Would it do any harm if he just took one close—?

COMMON sense took Hawkins by the scruff of the neck and yanked him over to the tool shed. He got out his pick and resolutely set off on a prospecting jaunt to a hummocky field that might yield some oxides. He was especially low on coppers.

The long walk left him sweating hard, with his lust for a peek into the kiln quiet in his breast. He swung his pick almost at random into one of the hummocks; it clanged on a stone, which he excavated. A largely obliterated inscription said:

ERSITY OF CHIC
OGICAL LABO
ELOVED MEMORY OF
KILLED IN ACT

The potter swore mildly. He had hoped the field would turn out to be a cemetery, preferably a once-fashionable cemetery full of once massive bronze caskets moldered into oxides of tin and copper.

WELL, hell, maybe there was some around anyway.

He headed lackadaisically for the second largest hillock and sliced into it with his pick. There was a stone to undercut and topple into a trench, and then the potter was very glad he'd stuck at it. His nostrils were filled with the bitter smell and the dirt was tinged with the exciting blue of copper salts. The pick went *clang!*

Hawkins, puffing, pried up a stainless steel plate that was quite badly stained and was also marked with incised letters. It seemed to have pulled loose from rotting bronze; there were rivets on the back that brought up flakes of green patina. The potter wiped off the surface dirt with his sleeve, turned it to catch the sunlight obliquely and read:

"HONEST JOHN BARLOW

"Honest John," famed in university annals, represents a challenge which medical science has not yet answered: revival of a human being accidentally thrown into a state of suspended animation.

In 1988 Mr. Barlow, a leading Evanston real estate dealer, visited his dentist for treatment of an impacted wisdom tooth. His dentist requested and received permission to use the experimental anesthetic Cycloparadimethanol-B-7, developed at the University.

After administration of the anesthetic, the dentist resorted to his drill. By freakish mischance, a short circuit in his machine delivered 220 volts of 60-cycle current into the patient. (In a damage suit instituted by Mrs.

Barlow against the dentist, the University and the makers of the drill, a jury found for the defendants.) Mr. Barlow never got up from the dentist's chair and was assumed to have died of poisoning, electrocution or both.

Morticians preparing him for embalming discovered, however, that their subject was—though certainly not living—just as certainly not dead. The University was notified and a series of exhaustive tests was begun, including attempts to duplicate the trance state on volunteers. After a bad run of seven cases which ended fatally, the attempts were abandoned.

Honest John was long an exhibit at the University museum, and livened many a football game as mascot of the University's Blue Crushers. The bounds of taste were overstepped, however, when a pledge to Sigma Delta Chi was ordered in '03 to "kidnap" Honest John from his loosely guarded glass museum case and introduce him into the Rachel Swanson Memorial Girls' Gymnasium shower room.

ON May 22nd, 2003, the University Board of Regents issued the following order: "By unanimous vote, it is directed that the remains of Honest John Barlow be removed from the University museum and conveyed to the University's Lieutenant James Scott III Memorial Biological Laboratories and there be securely locked in a specially prepared vault. It is further directed that all possible measures for the preservation of these remains be taken by the Laboratory administration and that access to these remains be denied to all persons except qualified scholars authorized in writing by the Board. The Board reluctantly takes this action in view of recent notices and photographs in the nation's press which, to say the least, reflect but small credit upon the University."

IT WAS far from his field, but Hawkins understood what had happened—an early and accidental blundering onto the bare bones of the Levantman shock anesthesia, which had since been replaced by other methods. To bring subjects out of Levantman shock, you let them have a squirt of simple saline in the trigeminal nerve. Interesting. And now about that bronze—

He heaved the pick into the rotting green salts, expecting no resistance, and almost fractured his wrist, *something* down there was *solid.* He began to flake off the oxides.

A half-hour of work brought him down to phosphor bronze, a huge casting of the almost incorruptible metal. It had weakened structurally over the centuries; he could fit the point of his pick under a corroded boss and pry off great creaking and grumbling striae of the stuff.

Hawkins wished he had an archeologist with him, but didn't dream of returning to his shop and calling one to take over the find. He was an all-around man: by choice and in his free time, an artist in clay and glaze; by necessity, an automotive, electronics and atomic engineer who could also swing a project in traffic control, individual and group psychology, architecture or tool design. He didn't yell for a specialist every time something out of his line came up; there were so few with so much to do...

He trenched around his find, discovering that it was a great brick-shaped bronze mass with an excitingly hollow sound. A long strip of moldering metal from one of the long vertical faces pulled away, exposing red rust that went *whoosh* and was sucked into the interior of the mass.

It had been de-aired, thought Hawkins, and there must have been an inner jacket of glass, which had crystallized through the centuries and quietly crumbled at the first clang of his pick. He didn't know what a vacuum would do to a subject of Levantman shock, but he had hopes, nor did he quite understand what a real estate dealer was, but it might have something to do with pottery. And *anything* might have a bearing on Topic Number One.

HE FLUNG his pick out of the trench, climbed out and set off at a dogtrot for his shop. A little rummaging turned up a hypo and there was a plasticontainer of salt in the kitchen.

Back at his dig, he chipped for another half-hour to expose the juncture of lid and body. The hinges were hopeless; he smashed them off.

Hawkins extended the telescopic handle of the pick for the best leverage, fitted its point into a deep pit, set its built-in fulcrum, and heaved. Five more heaves and he could see, inside the vault, what looked like a dusty marble statue. Ten more and he could see that it was the naked body of Honest John Barlow, Evanston real estate dealer, uncorrupted by time.

The potter found the apex of the trigeminal nerve with his needle's point and gave him 60 cc.

In an hour Barlow's chest began to pump.

In another hour, he rasped, "Did it work?"

"Did it!" muttered Hawkins.

Barlow opened his eyes and stirred, looked down, turned his hands before his eyes—

"I'll sue!" he screamed. "My clothes! My fingernails!" A horrid suspicion came over his face and he clapped his hands to his hairless scalp. "My hair!" he wailed. "I'll sue you for every penny you've got! That release won't mean a damned thing in court—I didn't sign away my hair and clothes and fingernails!"

"They'll grow back," said Hawkins casually. "Also your epidermis. Those parts of you weren't alive, you know, so they weren't preserved like the rest of you. I'm afraid the clothes are gone, though."

"What is this—the University hospital?" demanded Barlow. "I want a phone. No, you phone. Tell my wife I'm all right and tell Sam Immerman—he's my lawyer—to get over here right away. Greenleaf 7-4022. Ow!" He had tried to sit up, and a portion of his pink skin rubbed against the inner surface of the casket, which was powdered by the ancient crystallized glass. "What the hell did you guys do, boil me alive? Oh, you're going to pay for this."

"You're all right," said Hawkins, wishing now he had a reference book to clear up several obscure terms. "Your epidermis will start growing immediately. You're not in the hospital. Look here."

HE HANDED Barlow the stainless steel plate that had labeled the casket. After a suspicious glance, the man started to read. Finishing, he laid the plate carefully on the edge of the vault and was silent for a spell.

"Poor Verna," he said at last. "It doesn't say whether she was stuck with the court costs. Do you happen to know—"

"No," said the potter. "All I know is what was on the plate, and how to revive you. The dentist accidentally gave you a dose of what we call Levantman shock anesthesia. We haven't used it for centuries; it was powerful, but too dangerous."

"Centuries..." brooded the man. "Centuries...I'll bet Sam swindled her out of her eyeteeth. Poor Verna. How long ago was it? What year is this?"

Hawkins shrugged. "We call it 7-B-936. That's no help to you. It takes a long time for these metals to oxidize."

"Like that movie," Barlow muttered. "Who would have thought it? Poor Verna!" He blubbered and sniffled, reminding Hawkins powerfully of the fact that he had been found under a flat rock.

Almost angrily, the potter demanded, "How many children did you have?"

"None yet," sniffed Barlow. "My first wife didn't want them. But Verna wants one—wanted one—but we're going to wait until—we *were* going to wait until—"

"Of course," said the potter, feeling a savage desire to tell him off, blast him to hell and gone for his work. But he choked it down. There was The Problem to think of; there was always The Problem to think of, and this poor blubberer might unexpectedly supply a clue. Hawkins would have to pass him on.

"COME along," Hawkins said. "My time is short."

Barlow looked up, outraged. "How can you be so unfeeling? I'm a human being like—"

The Los Angeles-Chicago "rocket" thundered overhead and Barlow broke off in mid-complaint. "Beautiful!" he breathed, following it with his eyes. "Beautiful!"

He climbed out of the vault, too interested to be pained by its roughness against his infantile skin. "After all," he said briskly, "this should have its sunny side. I never was much for reading, but this is just like one of those stories. And I ought to make some money out of it, shouldn't I?" He gave Hawkins a shrewd glance.

"You want money?" asked the potter. "Here." He handed over a fistful of change and bills. "You'd better put my shoes on. It'll be about a quarter-mile. Oh, and you're—uh, modest?—yes, that was the word. Here." Hawkins gave him his pants, but Barlow was excitedly counting the money.

"Eighty-five, eighty-six—and it's dollars, too! I thought it'd be credits or whatever they call them. 'E Pluribus Unum' and 'Liberty'—just different faces. Say, is there a catch to this? Are these real, genuine, honest twenty-two-cent dollars like we had or just wallpaper?"

"They're quite all right, I assure you," said the potter. "I wish you'd come along. I'm in a hurry."

THE man babbled as they stumped toward the shop. "Where are we going—The Council of Scientists, the World Coordinator or something like that?"

"Who? Oh, no. We call them 'President' and 'Congress.' No, that wouldn't do any good at all. I'm just taking you to see some people."

"I ought to make plenty out of this. *Plenty!* I could write books. Get some smart young fellow to put it into words for me and I'll bet I could turn out a bestseller. What's the setup on things like that?"

"It's about like that. Smart young fellows. But there aren't any bestsellers any more. People don't read much nowadays. We'll find something equally profitable for you to do."

Back in the shop, Hawkins gave Barlow a suit of clothes, deposited him in the waiting room and called Central in Chicago. "Take him away," he pleaded. "I have time for one more firing and he blathers and blathers. I haven't told him anything. Perhaps we should just turn him loose and let him find his own level, but there's a chance—"

"The Problem," agreed Central. "Yes, there's a chance."

The potter delighted Barlow by making him a cup of coffee with a cube that not only dissolved in cold water but heated the water to boiling point. Killing time, Hawkins chatted about the "rocket" Barlow had admired, and had to haul himself up short; he had almost told the real estate man what its top speed really was—almost, indeed, revealed that it was not a rocket.

He regretted, too, that he had so casually handed Barlow a couple of hundred dollars. The man seemed obsessed with fear that they were worthless since Hawkins refused to take a note or I.O.U. or even a definite promise of repayment. But Hawkins couldn't go into details, and was very glad when a stranger arrived from Central.

"Tinny-Peete, from Algeciras," the stranger told him swiftly as the two of them met at the door. "Psychist for Poprob. Polasigned special overtake Barlow."

"Thank Heaven," said Hawkins. "Barlow," he told the man from the past, "this is Tinny-Peete. He's going to take care of you and help you make lots of money."

The psychist stayed for a cup of the coffee whose preparation had delighted Barlow, and then conducted the real estate man down the corduroy road to his car, leaving the potter to speculate on whether he could at last crack his kilns.

Hawkins, abruptly dismissing Barlow and the Problem, happily picked the chinking from around the door of the number two kiln, prying it open a trifle. A blast of heat and the heady, smoky scent of the reduction fire delighted him. He peered and saw a corner of a shelf glowing cherry-red, becoming obscured by wavering black areas as it lost heat through the opened door. He slipped a charred wood paddle under a mug on the shelf and pulled it out as a sample, the hairs on the back of his hand curling and scorching. The mug crackled and pinged and Hawkins sighed happily.

The bismuth resinate luster had fired to perfection, a haunting film of silvery-black metal with strange bluish lights in it as it turned before the eyes, and the Problem of Population seemed very far away to Hawkins then.

BARLOW and Tinny-Peete arrived at the concrete highway where the psychist's car was parked in a safety bay.

"What—a—*boat!*" gasped the man from the past.

"Boat? No, that's my car."

Barlow surveyed it with awe. Swept-back lines, deep-drawn compound curves, kilograms of chrome. He ran his hands futilely over the door—or was it the door?—in a futile search for a handle, and asked respectfully, "How fast does it go?"

The psychist gave him a keen look and said slowly, "Two hundred and fifty. You can tell by the speedometer."

"Wow! My old Chevvy could hit a hundred on a straightaway, but you're out of my class, mister!"

Tinny-Peete somehow got a huge, low door open and Barlow descended three steps into immense cushions, floundering over to the right. He was too fascinated to pay serious attention to his flayed dermis. The dashboard was a lovely wilderness of dials, plugs, indicators, lights, scales and switches.

The psychist climbed down into the driver's seat and did something with his feet. The motor started like lighting a blowtorch as big as a silo. Wallowing around in the cushions, Barlow saw through a rear-view mirror a tremendous exhaust filled with brilliant white sparkles.

"Do you like it?" yelled the psychist,

"It's terrific!" Barlow yelled back. "It's—"

He was shut up as the car pulled out from the bay into the road with a great *voo-ooo-ooom!* A gale roared past Barlow's head, though the windows seemed to be closed; the impression of speed was terrific. He located the speedometer on the dashboard and saw it climb past 90, 100, 150, 200.

"Fast enough for me," yelled the psychist, noting that Barlow's face fell in response. "Radio?"

He passed over a surprisingly light object like a football helmet, with no trailing wires, and pointed to a row of buttons. Barlow put on the helmet, glad to have the roar of air stilled, and pushed a pushbutton. It lit up satisfyingly and Barlow settled back even farther for a sample of the brave new world's super-modern taste in ingenious entertainment.

'TAKE IT AND STICK IT!" a voice roared in his ears.

HE SNATCHED off the helmet and gave the psychist an injured look. Tinny-Peete grinned and turned a dial associated with the pushbutton layout. The man from the past donned the helmet again and found the voice had lowered to normal.

"The show of shows! The super-show! The super-duper show! The quiz of quizzes! *Take it and stick it!*"

There were shrieks of laughter in the background.

"Here we got the contes-tants all ready to go. You know how we work it. I hand a contes-tant a triangle-shaped cutout and like that down the line. Now we got these here boards, they got cut-out places the same shape as the triangles and things, only they're all different shapes, and the first contes-tant that sticks the cutouts into the board, he wins.

"Now I'm gonna innaview the first contes-tant. Right here, honey. What's your name?"

"Name? Uh—"

"Hoddaya like that, folks? She don't remember her name! Hah? *Would you buy that for a quater?*" The question was spoken with arch significance, and the audience shrieked, howled and whistled its appreciation.

It was dull listening when you didn't know the punch lines and catch lines. Barlow pushed another button, with his free hand ready at the volume control.

"—latest from Washington. It's about Senator Hull-Mendoza. He is still attacking the Bureau of Fisheries. The North California Syndicalist says he got affidavits that John

Kingsley-Schultz is a bluenose from way back. He didn't publistat the affydavits, but he says they say that Kingsley-Schultz was saw at bluenose meetings in Oregon State College and later at Florida University. Kingsley-Schultz says he gotta confess he did major in fly-casting at Oregon and got his Ph.D. in game fish at Florida.

"And here is a quote from Kingsley-Schultz: 'Hull-Mendoza don't know what he's talking about. He should drop dead.' Unquote. Hull-Mendoza says he won't publistat the affydavits to pertect his sources. He says they was sworn by three former employes of the Bureau which was fired for in-competence and in-com-pat-ibility by Kingsley-Schultz.

"Elsewhere they was the usual run of traffic accidents. A three-way pileup of cars on Route 66 going outta Chicago took twelve lives. The Chicago-Los Angeles morning rocket crashed and exploded in the Mo-have—Mo-javvy—whatever-you-call-it Desert. All the 94 people aboard got killed. A Civil Aeronautics Authority investigator on the scene says that the pilot was buzzing herds of sheep and didn't pull out in time.

"Hey! Here's a hot one from New York! A Diesel tug run wild in the harbor while the crew was below and shoved in the port bow of the luck-shury liner *S. S. Placentia*. It says the ship filled and sank taking the lives of an es-timated 180 passengers and 50 crew members. Six divers was sent down to study the wreckage, but they died, too, when their suits turned out to be fulla little holes.

"And here is a bulletin I just gat from Denver. It seems—"

BARLOW took off the headset uncomprehendingly. "He seemed so callous," he yelled at the driver. "I was listening to a newscast—"

Tinny-Peete shook his head and pointed at his ears. The roar of air was deafening. Barlow frowned baffledly and stared out of the window.

A glowing sign said:

MOOGS!
WOULD YOU BUY IT
FOR A QUARTER?

He didn't know what Moogs was or were; the illustration showed an incredibly proportioned girl, 99.9 percent naked, writhing passionately in animated full color.

The roadside jingle was still with him, but with a new feature. Radar or something spotted the car and alerted the lines of the jingle. Each in turn sped along a roadside track, even with the car, so it could be read before the next line was alerted.

IF THERE'S A GIRL
YOU WANT TO GET
DEFLOCCULIZE
UNROMANTIC SWEAT.
"A*R*M*P*I*T*T*O"

Another animated job, in two panels, the familiar "Before and After." The first said, "Just Any Cigar?" and was illustrated with a two-person domestic tragedy of a wife holding her nose while her coarse and red-faced husband puffed a slimy-looking rope. The second panel glowed, "Or a VUELTA ABAJO?" and was illustrated with—

Barlow blushed and looked at his feet until they had passed the sign.

"Coming into Chicago!" bawled Tinny-Peete.

Other cars were showing up, all of them dreamboats.

Watching them, Barlow began to wonder if he knew what a kilometer was, exactly. They seemed to be traveling so slowly, if you ignored the roaring air past your ears and didn't let the speedy lines of the dreamboats fool you. He would have sworn they were really crawling along at twenty-five, with occasional spurts up to thirty. How much was a kilometer, anyway?

The city loomed ahead, and it was just what it ought to be: towering skyscrapers, overhead ramps, landing platforms for helicopters—

He clutched at the cushions. Those two 'copters. They were going to—they were going to—they—

He didn't see what happened because their apparent collision courses took them behind a giant building.

SCREAMINGLY sweet blasts of sound surrounded them as they stopped for a red light. "What the hell is going on here?" said Barlow in a shrill, frightened voice, because the braking time was just about zero, he wasn't hurled against the dashboard. "Who's kidding who?"

"Why, what's the matter?" demanded the driver.

The light changed to green and he started the pickup. Barlow stiffened as he realized that the rush of air past his ears began just a brief, unreal split-second before the car was actually moving. He grabbed for the door handle on his side.

The city grew on them slowly: scattered buildings, denser buildings, taller buildings, and a red light ahead. The car rolled to a stop in zero braking time, the rush of air cut off an instant after it stopped, and Barlow was out of the car and running frenziedly down a sidewalk one instant after that.

They'll track me down, he thought, panting. It's a secret police thing. They'll get you—mind reading machines, television eyes everywhere, afraid you'll tell their slaves about freedom and stuff. They don't let anybody cross them, like that story I once read.

Winded, he slowed to a walk and congratulated himself that he had guts enough not to turn around. That was what they always watched for. Walking, he was just another business-suited back among hundreds. He would be safe, he would be safe—

A hand tumbled from a large, coarse, handsome face thrust close to his: "Wassamatta bumpinninna people likeya owna sidewalk gotta miner slamya inn a mushya bassar!" It was neither the mad potter nor the mad driver.

"Excuse me, said Barlow. "What did you say?"

"Oh, yeah?" yelled the stranger dangerously, and waited for an answer.

Barlow, with the feeling that he had somehow been suckered into the short end of an intricate land-title deal, heard himself reply belligerently, "Yeah!"

The stranger let go of his shoulder and snarled, "Oh, yeah?"

"Yeah!" said Barlow, yanking his jacket back into shape.

"Aaah!" snarled the stranger with more contempt and disgust than ferocity. He added an obscenity current in Barlow's time, a standard but physiologically impossible directive, and strutted off hulking his shoulders and balling his fists.

BARLOW walked on, trembling. Evidently he had handled it well enough. He stopped at a red light while the long, low dreamboats roared before him and pedestrians in the sidewalk flow with him threaded their ways through the stream of cars. Brakes screamed, fenders clanged and dented, hoarse cries flew back and forth between drivers and walkers. He leaped backward frantically as one car swerved over an arc of sidewalk to miss another.

The signal changed to green, the cars kept on coming for about thirty seconds and then dwindled to an occasional light-runner. Barlow crossed warily and leaned against a vending machine, blowing big breaths.

Look natural, he told himself. *Do something normal. Buy something from the machine.*

He fumbled out some change, got a newspaper for a dime, a handkerchief for a quarter and a candy bar for another quarter.

The faint chocolate smell made him ravenous suddenly. He clawed at the glassy wrapper printed "CRIGGLIES" quite futilely for a few seconds, and then it divided neatly by itself. The bar made three good bites, and he bought two more and gobbled them down.

Thirsty, he drew a carbonated orange drink in another one of the glassy wrappers from the machine for another dime. When he fumbled with it, it divided neatly and spilled all over his knees. Barlow decided he had been there long enough and walked on.

The shop windows were—shop windows. People still wore and bought clothes, still smoked and bought tobacco, still ate and bought food. And they still went to the movies, he saw with pleased surprise as he passed and then returned to a glittering place whose sign said it was THE BIJOU.

The place seemed to be showing a quintuple feature, *Babies Are Terrible, Don't Have Children,* and *The Canali Kid.*

It was irresistible; he paid a dollar and went in.

He caught the tail end of *The Canali Kid* in three-dimensional, full-color, full-scent production. It appeared to be an interplanetary saga winding up with a chase scene and a reconciliation between estranged hero and heroine. *Babies Are Terrible* and *Don't Have Children* were fantastic arguments against parenthood—the grotesquely exaggerated dangers of painfully graphic childbirth, vicious children, old parents beaten and starved by their sadistic offspring. The audience, Barlow astoundedly noted, was placidly champing sweets and showing no particular signs of revulsion.

The *Coming Attractions* drove him into the lobby. The fanfares were shattering, the blazing colors blinding, and the added scents stomach-heaving.

WHEN his eyes again became accustomed to the moderate lighting of the lobby, he groped his way to a bench and opened the newspaper he had bought. It turned out to be *The Racing Sheet,* which afflicted him with a crushing sense of loss. The familiar boxed index in the lower left hand corner of the front page showed almost unbearably that Churchill Downs and Empire City were still in business—

Blinking back tears, he turned to the Past Performances at Churchill. They weren't using abbreviations any more, and the pages because of that were single column instead of double. But it was all the same—or was it?

He squinted at the first race, a three-quarter-mile maiden claimer for thirteen hundred dollars. Incredibly, the track record was two minutes, ten and three-fifths seconds. Any beetle in his time could have knocked off the three-quarter in one-fifteen. It was the same for the other distances, much worse for route events.

What the hell had happened to everything?

He studied the form of a five-year-old brown mare in the second and couldn't make head or tail of it. She'd won and lost and placed and showed and lost and placed without rhyme or reason. She looked like a front-runner for a couple of races and then she looked like a no-good pig and then she looked like a mudder but the next time it rained she wasn't and then she was a stayer and then she was a pig again. In a good five-thousand-dollar allowances event, too!

Barlow looked at the other entries and it slowly dawned on him that they were all like the five-year-old brown mare. Not a single damned horse running had the slightest trace of class.

Somebody sat down beside him and said, "that's the story."

BARLOW whirled to his feet and saw it was Tinny-Peete, his driver.

"I was in doubts about telling you," said the psychist, "but I see you have some growing suspicions of the truth. Please don't get excited. It's all right, I tell you."

"So you've got me," said Barlow.

"Got you?"

"Don't pretend. I can put two and two together. You're the secret police. You and the rest of the aristocrats live in luxury on the sweat of these oppressed slaves. You're afraid of me because you have to keep them ignorant."

There was a bellow of bright laughter from the psychist that got them blank looks from other patrons of the lobby. The laughter didn't sound at all sinister.

"Let's get out of here," said Tinny-Peete, still chuckling. "You couldn't possibly have it more wrong." He engaged

Barlow's arm and led him to the street. "The actual truth is that the millions of workers live in luxury on the sweat of the handful of aristocrats. I shall probably die before my time of overwork unless—" He gave Barlow a speculative look. "You may be able to help us."

"I know that gag," sneered Barlow. "I made money in my time and to make money you have to get people on your side. Go ahead and shoot me if you want, but you're not going to make a fool out of me."

"You nasty little ingrate!" snapped the psychist, with a kaleidoscopic change of mood. "This damned mess is all your fault and the fault of people like you! Now come along and no more of your nonsense."

He yanked Barlow into an office building lobby and an elevator that, disconcertingly, went *whoosh* loudly as it rose. The real estate man's knees were wobbly as the psychist pushed him from the elevator, down a corridor and into an office.

A hawk-faced man rose from a plain chair as the door closed behind them. After an angry look at Barlow, he asked the psychist, "Was I called from the Pole to inspect this—this—?"

"Unget updandered. I've dee-probed etfind quasichance exhim Poprobattackline," said the psychist soothingly.

"Doubt," grunted the hawk-faced man.

"Try," suggested Tinny-Peete.

"Very well. Mr. Barlow, I understand you and your lamented had no children."

"What of it?"

"This of it. You were a blind, selfish stupid ass to tolerate economic and social conditions which penalized childbearing by the prudent and foresighted. You made us what we are today, and I want you to know that we are far from satisfied. Damnfool rockets! Damn-fool automobiles! Damn-fool cities with overhead ramps!"

"As far as I can see," said Barlow, "you're running down the best features of time. Are you crazy?"

"The rockets aren't rockets. They're turbo-jets—good turbo-jets, but the fancy shell around them makes for a bad drag. The automobiles have a top speed of one hundred kilometers per hour—a kilometer is, if I recall my paleolinguistics, three-fifths of a mile—and the speedometers are all rigged accordingly so the drivers will think they're going two hundred and fifty. The cities are ridiculous, expensive, unsanitary, wasteful conglomerations of people who'd be better off and more productive if they were spread over the countryside.

"We need the rockets and trick speedometers and cities because, while you and your kind were being prudent and foresighted and not having children, the migrant workers, slum dwellers and tenant farmers were shiftlessly and shortsightedly having children—breeding, breeding. My God, how they bred!"

"WAIT a minute," objected Barlow. "There were lots of people in our crowd who had two or three children."

"The attrition of accidents, illness, wars and such took care of that. Your intelligence was bred out. It is gone. Children that should have been born never were. The just-average, they'll-get-along majority took over the population. The average IQ now is 45."

"But that's far in the future—"

"So are you," grunted the hawk-faced man sourly.

"But who are *you* people?"

"Just people—real people. Some generations ago, the geneticists realized at last that nobody was going to pay any attention to what they said, so they abandoned words for deeds. Specifically, they formed and recruited for a closed corporation intended to maintain and improve the breed. We are their descendants, about three million of us. There are five billion of the others, so we are their slaves.

"During the past couple of years I've designed a skyscraper, kept Billings Memorial Hospital here in Chicago running, headed off war with Mexico and directed traffic at LaGuardia Field in New York."

"I don't understand! Why don't you let them go to hell in their own way?"

The man grimaced. "We tried it once for three months. We holed up at the South Pole and waited. They didn't notice it. Some drafting-room people were missing, some chief nurses didn't show up, minor government people on the non-policy level couldn't be located. It didn't seem to matter.

"In a week there was hunger. In two weeks there were famine and plague, in three weeks war and anarchy. We called off the experiment; it took us most of the next generation to get things squared away again."

"But why *didn't* you let them kill each other off?"

"Five billion corpses mean about five hundred million tons of rotting flesh."

Barlow had another idea. "Why don't you sterilize them?"

"Two and one-half billion operations is a lot of operations. Because they breed continuously, the job would never be done."

"I see. Like the marching Chinese!"

"Who the devil are they?"

"It was a—uh—paradox of my time. Somebody figured out that if all the Chinese in the world were to line up four abreast, I think it was, and start marching past a given point, they'd never stop because of the babies that would be born and grow up before they passed the point."

"That's right. Only instead of 'a given point,' make it 'the largest conceivable number of operating rooms that we could build and staff.' There could never be enough."

"Say!" said Barlow. "Those movies about babies—was that your propaganda?"

"It was. It doesn't seem to mean a thing to them. We have abandoned the idea of attempting propaganda contrary to a biological drive."

"So if you work *with* a biological drive—?"

"I know of none which is consistent with inhibition of fertility."

BARLOW'S face went poker-blank, the result of years of careful discipline. "You don't, huh? You're the great brains and you can't think of any?"

"Why, no," said the psychist innocently. "Can you?"

"That depends. I sold ten thousand acres of Siberian tundra—through a dummy firm, of course—after the partition of Russia. The buyers thought they were getting improved building lots on the outskirts of Kiev. I'd say that was a lot tougher than this job."

"How so?" asked the hawk-faced man.

"Those were normal, suspicious customers and these are morons, born suckers. You just figure out a con they'll fall for; they won't know enough to do any smart checking."

The psychist and the hawk-faced man had also had training; they kept themselves from looking with sudden hope at each other.

"You seem to have something in mind," said the psychist.

Barlow's poker face went blanker still. "Maybe I have. I haven't heard any offer yet."

"There's the satisfaction of knowing that you've prevented Earth's resources from being so plundered," the hawk-faced man pointed out, "that the race will soon become extinct. "

"I don't know that," Barlow said bluntly. "All I have is your word."

"If you really have a method, I don't think any price would be too great," the psychist offered.

"Money," said Barlow.

"All you want."

"More than you want," the hawk-faced man corrected.

"Prestige," added Barlow. "Plenty of publicity. My picture and my name in the papers and over TV every day, statues to me, parks and cities and streets and other things named after me. A whole chapter in the history books."

The psychist made a facial sign to the hawk-faced man that meant, "Oh, brother!"

The hawk-faced man signaled back, "Steady, boy!"

"It's not too much to ask," the psychist agreed.

Barlow, sensing a seller's market, said, "Power!"

"Power?" the hawk-faced man repeated puzzledly. "Your own hydro station or nuclear pile?"

"I mean a world dictatorship with me as dictator!"

"Well, now—" said the psychist, but the hawk-faced man interrupted, "It would take a special emergency act of Congress but the situation warrants it. I think that can be guaranteed."

"Could you give us some indication of your plan?" the psychist asked.

"Ever hear of lemmings?"

"No."

"They are—were, I guess, since you haven't heard of them— little animals in Norway, and every few years they'd swarm to the coast and swim out to sea until they drowned. I figure on putting some lemming urge into the population."

"How?"

"I'll save that till I get the right signatures on the deal."

THE hawk-faced man said, "I'd like to work with you on it, Barlow. My name's Ryan-Ngana." He put out his hand.

Barlow looked closely at the hand, then at the man's face. "Ryan what?"

"Ngana."

"That sounds like an African name."

"It is. My mother's father was a Watusi."

Barlow didn't take the hand. "I thought you looked pretty dark. I don't want to hurt your feelings, but I don't think I'd be at my best working with you. There must be somebody else just as well qualified, I'm sure."

The psychist made a facial sign to Ryan-Ngana that meant, "Steady *yourself,* boy!"

"Very well," Ryan-Ngana told Barlow. "We'll see what arrangement can be made."

"It's not that I'm prejudiced, you understand. Some of my best friends—"

"Mr. Barlow, don't give it another thought. Anybody who could pick on the lemming analogy is going to be useful to us."

And so he would, thought Ryan-Ngana, alone in the office after Tinny-Peete had taken Barlow up to the helicopter stage. So he would. Poprob had exhausted every rational attempt and the new Poprobattacklines would have to be irrational or sub-rational. This creature from the past with his lemming legends and his improved building lots would be a fountain of precious vicious self-interest.

Ryan-Ngana sighed and stretched. He had to go and run the San Francisco subway. Summoned early from the Pole to study Barlow, he'd left unfinished a nice little theorem. Between interruptions, he was slowly constructing an n-dimensional geometry whose foundations and superstructure owed no debt whatsoever to intuition.

UPSTAIRS, waiting for a helicopter, Barlow was explaining to Tinny-Peete that he had nothing against Negroes, and Tinny-Peete wished he had some of Ryan-Ngana's imperturbability and humor for the ordeal.

The helicopter took them to International Airport where, Tinny-Peete explained, Barlow would leave for the Pole.

The man from the past wasn't sure he'd like a dreary waste of ice and cold.

"It's all right," said the psychist. "A civilized layout. Warm, pleasant. You'll be able to work more efficiently there. All the facts at your fingertips, a good secretary—."

"I'll need a pretty big staff," said Barlow, who had learned from thousands of deals never to take the first offer.

"I meant a private, confidential one," said Tinny-Peete readily, "but you can have as many as you want. You'll naturally have top-primary-top priority if you really have a workable plan."

"Let's not forget this dictatorship angle," said Barlow.

He didn't know that the psychist would just as readily have promised him deification to get him happily on the "rocket" for the Pole. Tinny-Peete had no wish to be torn limb from limb; he knew very well that it would end that way if the population learned from this anachronism that there was a small elite which considered itself head, shoulders, trunk and groin above the rest. The fact that this assumption was perfectly true and the fact that the elite was condemned by its superiority to a life of the most grinding toil would not be considered; the difference would.

The psychist finally put Barlow aboard the "rocket" with some thirty people—real people—headed for the Pole.

BARLOW was airsick all the way because of a post-hypnotic suggestion Tinny-Peete had planted in him. One idea was to make him as averse as possible to a return trip, and another idea was to spare the other passengers from his aggressive, talkative company.

Barlow during the first day at the pole was reminded of his first day in the Army. It was the same now-where-the-hell-are-we-going-to-put-*you?* business until he took a firm line with them. Then instead of acting like supply sergeants they acted like hotel clerks.

It was a wonderful, wonderfully calculated buildup, and one that he failed to suspect. After all, in his time a visitor from the past would have been lionized.

At day's end he reclined in a snug underground billet with the 60-mile gales roaring yards overhead, and tried to put two and two together.

It was like old times, he thought—like a coup in real estate where you had the competition by the throat, like a 50-percent rent boost when you knew damned well there was no place for the tenants to move, like smiling when you read over the breakfast orange juice that the city council had decided to build a school on the ground you had acquired by a deal with the city council. And it was simple. He would just sell tundra building lots to eagerly suicidal lemmings, and that was absolutely all there was to solving the Problem that had these double-domes spinning.

They'd have to work out most of the details, naturally, but what the hell, that was what subordinates were for. He'd need specialists in advertising, engineering, communications—did they know anything about hypnotism? That might be helpful. If not, there'd have to be a lot of bribery done, but he'd make sure—damned sure—there were unlimited funds.

Just selling building lots to lemmings...

He wished, as he fell asleep, that poor Verna could have been in on this. It was his biggest, most stupendous deal. Verna—that sharp shyster Sam Immerman must have swindled her...

IT BEGAN the next day with people coming to visit him. He knew the approach. They merely wanted to be helpful to their illustrious visitor from the past and would he help fill them in about his era, which unfortunately was somewhat obscure historically, and what did he think could be done about the Problem? He told them he was too old to be roped any more, and they wouldn't get any information out of him until he got a letter of intent from at least the Polar President, and a session of the Polar Congress empowered to make him dictator.

He got the letter and the session. He presented his program, was asked whether his conscience didn't revolt at its callousness, explained succinctly that a deal was a deal and anybody who wasn't smart enough to protect himself didn't deserve protection—"Caveat emptor," he threw in for scholarship, and had to translate it to "Let the buyer beware." He didn't, he stated, give a damn about either the morons or their intelligent slaves; he'd told them his price and that was all he was interested in.

Would they meet it or wouldn't they?

The Polar President offered to resign in his favor, with certain temporary emergency powers that the Polar Congress would vote him if he thought them necessary. Barlow demanded the title of World Dictator, complete control of world finances, salary to be decided by himself, and the publicity campaign and historical write-up to begin at once.

"As for the emergency powers," he added, "they are neither to be temporary nor limited."

Somebody wanted the floor to discuss the matter, with the declared hope that perhaps Barlow would modify his demands.

"You've got the proposition," Barlow said. "I'm not knocking off even ten percent."

"But what if the Congress refuses, sir?" the President asked.

"Then you can stay up here at the Pole and try to work it out yourselves. I'll get what I want from the morons. A shrewd operator like me doesn't have to compromise; I haven't got a single competitor in this whole cockeyed moronic era."

Congress waived debate and voted by show of hands. Barlow won unanimously.

"You don't know how close you came to losing me," he said in his first official address to the joint Houses. "I'm not the boy to haggle; either I get what I ask for I go elsewhere. The first thing I want is to see designs for a new palace for me—nothing *un*ostentatious, either—and your best painters and sculptors to start working on my portraits and statues. Meanwhile, I'll get my staff together."

He dismissed the Polar President and the Polar Congress, telling them that he'd let them know when the next meeting would be.

A week later, the program started with North America the first target.

Mrs. Garvy was resting after dinner before the ordeal of turning on the dishwasher. The TV, of course, was on and it said: "Ooooh!"—long, shuddery and ecstatic, the cue for the *Parfume Assault Criminale* spot commercial. "Girls," said the announcer hoarsely, "do you want your man? It's easy to get him—easy as a trip to Venus."

"Huh?" said Mrs. Garvy.

"Wassamatter?" snorted her husband, starting out of a doze. "Ja hear that?"

"Wha'?"

"He said 'easy like a trip to Venus.' "

"So?"

"Well, I thought ya couldn't get to Venus. I thought they just had that one rocket thing that crashed on the Moon."

"Aah, women don't keep up with the news," said Garvy righteously, subsiding again.

"Oh," said his wife uncertainly.

And the next day, on *Henry's Other Mistress*, there was a new character who had just breezed in: Buzz Rentshaw, Master Rocket Pilot of the Venus run. On *Henry's Other Mistress*, "the broadcast drama about you and your neighbors, *folksy* people, *ordinary* people, *real* people!" Mrs. Garvy listened with amazement over a cooling cup of coffee as Buzz made hay of her hazy convictions.

MONA: Darling, it's so good to see you again!

BUZZ: You don't know how I've missed you on that dreary Venus run.

SOUND: *Venetian blind run down, key turned in door lock.*

MONA: Was it *very* dull, dearest?

BUZZ: Let's not talk about my humdrum job, darling. Let's talk about us.

SOUND: *Creaking bed.*

Well, the program was back to normal at last. That evening Mrs. Garvy tried to ask again whether her husband was sure about those rockets, but he was dozing right through *Take It and Stick It*, so she watched the screen and forgot the puzzle.

She was still rocking with laughter at the gag line, "Would you buy it for a quarter?" when the commercial went on for the detergent powder she always faithfully loaded her dishwasher with on the first of every month.

THE announcer displayed mountains of suds from a tiny piece of the stuff and coyly added: "Of course, Cleano don't lay around for you to pick up like the soap root on Venus, but it's pretty cheap and it's almost pretty near just as good. So for us plain folks who ain't lucky enough to live up there on Venus, Cleano is the real cleaning stuff!"

Then the chorus went into their "Cleano-is-the-stuff" jingle, but Mrs. Garvy didn't hear it. She was a stubborn woman, but it occurred to her that she was very sick indeed. She didn't want to worry her husband. The next day she quietly made an appointment with her family freud.

In the waiting room she picked up a fresh new copy of *Readers Pablum* and put it down with a faint palpitation. The lead article, according to the table of contents on the cover, was titled "The Most Memorable Venusian I Ever Met."

"The freud will see you now," said the nurse, and Mrs. Garvy tottered into his office.

His traditional glasses and whiskers were reassuring. She choked out the ritual: "Freud, forgive me, for I have neuroses."

He chanted the antiphonal: "Tut, my dear girl, what seems to be the trouble?"

"I got like a hole in the head," she quavered. "I seem to forget all kinds of things. Things like everybody seems to know and I don't."

"Well, that happens to everybody occasionally, my dear. I suggest a vacation on Venus."

The freud stared, open-mouthed, at the empty chair. His nurse came in and demanded, "Hey, you see how she scrammed? What was the matter with *her?*"

He took off his glasses and whiskers meditatively. "You can search me. I told her she should maybe try a vacation on Venus." A momentary bafflement came into his face and he dug through his desk drawers until he found a copy of the four-color, profusely illustrated journal of his profession. It had come that morning and he had lip-read it, though looking mostly at the pictures. He leafed through to the article *Advantages of the Planet Venus in Rest Cures.*

"It's right there," he said.

The nurse looked. "It sure is," she agreed. "Why shouldn't it be?"

"The trouble with these here neurotics," decided the freud, "is that they all the time got to fight reality. Show in the next twitch."

He put on his glasses and whiskers again and forgot Mrs. Garvy and her strange behavior.

"Freud, forgive me, for I have neuroses. "

"Tut, my dear girl, what seems to be the trouble?"

LIKE many cures of mental disorders, Mrs. Garvy's was achieved largely by self-treatment. She disciplined herself sternly out of the crazy notion that there had been only one rocket ship and that one a failure. She could join without wincing, eventually, in any conversation on the desirability of Venus as a place to retire, on its fabulous floral profusion. Finally she went to Venus.

All her friends were trying to book passage with the Evening Star Travel and Real Estate Corporation, but naturally the demand was crushing. She considered herself lucky to get a seat at last for the two-week summer cruise. The space ship took off from a place called Los Alamos, New Mexico. It looked just like all the spaceships on television and in the picture magazines, but was more comfortable than you would expect.

Mrs. Garvy was delighted with the fifty or so fellow-passengers assembled before takeoff. They were from all over the country and she had a distinct impression that they were on the brainy side. The captain, a tall, hawk-faced, impressive fellow named Ryan-Something or other, welcomed them aboard and trusted that their trip would be a memorable one. He regretted that there would be nothing to see because, "due to the meteorite season," the ports would be dogged down. It was disappointing, yet reassuring that the line was taking no chances.

There was the expected momentary discomfort at takeoff and then two monotonous days of droning travel through space to be whiled away in the lounge at cards or craps. The landing was a routine bump and the voyagers were issued tablets to swallow to immunize them against any minor ailments. When the tablets took effect, the lock was opened and Venus was theirs.

It looked much like a tropical island on Earth, except for a blanket of cloud overhead. But it had a heady, other-worldly quality that was intoxicating and glamorous.

The ten days of the vacation were suffused with a hazy magic. The soap root, as advertised, was free and sudsy. The fruits, mostly tropical varieties transplanted from Earth, were delightful. The simple shelters provided by the travel company were more than adequate for the balmy days and nights.

It was with sincere regret that the voyagers filed again into the ship, and swallowed more tablets doled out to counteract and sterilize any Venus illnesses they might unwittingly communicate to Earth.

VACATIONING was one thing. Power politics was another.

At the Pole, a small man was in a soundproof room, his face deathly pale and his body limp in a straight chair.

In the American Senate Chamber, Senator Hull-Mendoza (Synd., N. Cal.) was saying: "Mr. President and gentlemen, I would be remiss in my duty as a legislature if'n I didn't bring to the attention of the au-gust body I see here a perilous situation which is fraught with peril. As is well known to members of this au-gust body, the perfection of space flight has brought with it a situation I can only describe as fraught with peril. Mr. President and gentlemen, now that swift American rockets now traverse the trackless void of space between this planet and our nearest planetarial neighbor in space—and, gentlemen, I refer to Venus, the star of dawn, the brightest jewel in fair Vulcan's diadome—now, I say, I want to inquire what steps are being taken to colonize Venus with a vanguard of patriotic citizens like those minutemen of yore.

"Mr. President and gentlemen! There are in this world nations, envious nations—I do not name Mexico—who by fair means or foul may seek to wrest from Columbia's grasp the torch of freedom of space; nations whose low living standards and innate depravity give them an unfair advantage over the citizens of our fair republic.

"This is my program: I suggest that a city of more than 100,000 population be selected by lot. The citizens of the fortunate city are to be awarded choice lands on Venus free and clear, to have and to hold and convey to their descendants. And the national government shall provide free transportation to Venus for these citizens. And this program shall continue, city by city, until there has been deposited on Venus a sufficient vanguard of citizens to protect our manifest rights in that planet.

"Objections will be raised, for carping critics we have always with us. They will say there isn't enough steel. They will call it a cheap giveaway. I say there *is* enough steel for *one* city's population to be transferred to Venus, and that is all that is needed. For when the time comes for the second city to be transferred, the first, emptied city can be wrecked for the needed steel! And is it a giveaway? Yes! It is the most glorious giveaway in the history of mankind! Mr. President and gentlemen, there is no time to waste—Venus must be American!"

BLACK-KUPPERMAN, at the Pole, opened his eyes and said feebly, "The style was a little uneven. Do you think anybody'll notice?"

"You did fine, boy; just fine," Barlow reassured him.

Hull-Mendoza's bill became law.

Drafting machines at the South Pole were busy around the clock and the Pittsburgh steel mills spewed millions of plates into the Los Alamos spaceport of the Evening Star Travel and Real Estate Corporation. It was going to be Los Angeles, for logistic reasons, and the three most accomplished psycho-kineticists went to Washington and mingled in the crowd at the drawing to make certain that the Los Angeles capsule slithered into the fingers of the blindfolded Senator.

Los Angeles loved the idea and a forest of spaceships began to blossom in the desert. They weren't very good space ships, but they didn't have to be.

A team at the Pole worked at Barlow's direction on a mail setup. There would have to be letters to and from Venus to keep the slightest taint of suspicion from arising. Luckily Barlow remembered that the problem had been solved once before—by Hitler. Relatives of persons incinerated in the furnaces of Lublin or Majdanek continued to get cheery postal cards.

THE Los Angeles flight went off on schedule, under tremendous press, newsreel and television coverage. The world cheered the gallant Angelenos who were setting off on their patriotic voyage to the land of milk and honey. The forest of spaceships thundered up, and up, and out of sight without untoward incident. Billions envied the Angelenos, cramped and on short rations though they were.

Wreckers from San Francisco, whose capsule came up second, moved immediately into the city of the angels for the scrap steel their own flight would require. Senator Hull-Mendoza's constituents could do no less.

The president of Mexico, hypnotically alarmed at this extension of *yanqui imperialismo* beyond the stratosphere, launched his own Venus-colony program.

Across the water it was England versus Ireland, France versus Germany, China versus Russia, India versus Indonesia. Ancient hatreds grew into the flame's that were rocket ships assailing the air by hundreds daily.

Dear Ed, how are you? Sam and I are fine and hope you are fine. Is it nice up there like they say with food and close grone on trees? I drove by Springfield yesterday and it sure looked funny all the buildings down but of coarse it is worth it we have to keep the greasers in their place. Do you have any truble with them on Venus? Drop me a line some time. Your loving sister, Alma.

Dear Alma, I am fine and hope you are fine. It is a fine place here fine climate and easy living. The doctor told me today that I seem to be ten years younger. He thinks there is something in the air here keeps people young. We do not have much trouble with the greasers here they keep to theirselves it is just a question of us outnumbering them and staking out the best places for the Americans. In South Bay I know a nice little island that I have been saving for you and Sam with lots of blanket trees and ham bushes. Hoping to see you and Sam soon, your loving brother, Ed.

Sam and Alma were on their way shortly.

Poprob got a dividend in every nation after the emigration had passed the halfway mark. The lonesome stay-at-homes were unable to bear the melancholy of a low population density; their conditioning had been to swarms of their kin. After that point it was possible to foist off the crudest stripped-down accommodations on would-be emigrants; they didn't care.

Black-Kupperman did a final job on President Hull-Mendoza, the last job that genius of hypnotics would ever do on any moron, important or otherwise.

Hull-Mendoza, panic-stricken by his presidency over an emptying nation, joined his constituents. The *Independence,* aboard which traveled the national government of America, was the most elaborate of all the spaceships—bigger, more comfortable, with a lounge that was handsome, though cramped, and cloakrooms for Senators and Representatives. It went, however, to the same place as the others and Black-Kupperman killed himself, leaving a note that stated he "couldn't live with my conscience."

THE day after the American President departed, Barlow flew into a rage. Across his specially built desk were supposed to flow all Poprob high-level documents and this thing—this outrageous thing—called Poprob*term* apparently had got into the executive stage before he had even had a glimpse of it!

He buzzed for Rogge-Smith, his statistician. Rogge-Smith seemed to be at the bottom of it. Poprobterm seemed to be about first and second and third derivatives, whatever they were. Barlow had a deep distrust of anything more complex than what he called an "average."

While Rogge-Smith was still at the door, Barlow snapped, "What's the meaning of this? Why haven't I been consulted? How far have you people got and why have you been working on something I haven't authorized?"

"Didn't want to bother you, Chief," said Rogge-Smith. "It was really a technical matter, kind of a final cleanup. Want to come and see the work?"

Mollified, Barlow followed his statistician down the corridor.

"You still shouldn't have gone ahead without my okay," he grumbled. "Where the hell would you people have been without me?"

"That's right, Chief. We couldn't have swung it ourselves; our minds just don't work that way. And all that stuff you knew from Hitler—it wouldn't have occurred to us. Like poor Black-Kupperman."

They were in a fair-sized machine shop at the end of a slight upward incline. It was cold. Rogge-Smith pushed a button that started a motor, and a flood of arctic light poured in as the roof parted slowly. It showed a small spaceship with the door open.

BARLOW gaped as Rogge-Smith took him by the elbow and his other boys appeared: Swenson-Swenson, the engineer; Tsutsugimushi-Duncan, his propellants man; Kalb-French, advertising.

"In you go, Chief," said Tsutsugimushi-Duncan. "This is Poprobterm."

"But I'm the world Dictator!"

"You bet, Chief. You'll be in history, all right—but this is necessary, I'm afraid."

The door was closed. Acceleration slammed Barlow cruelly to the metal floor. Something broke and warm, wet stuff, salty-tasting, ran from his mouth to his chin. Arctic sunlight through a port suddenly became a fierce lancet stabbing at his eyes; he was out of the atmosphere.

Lying twisted and broken under the acceleration, Barlow realized that some things had not changed, that Jack Ketch was never asked to dinner however many shillings you paid him to do your dirty work, that murder will out, that crime pays only temporarily.

The last thing he learned was that death is the end of pain.

THE END

The Frogs of Mars

By ROGER DEE

The little guy comes into the bar just as the first Marscast is about to start. He scoffs at scientific facts and keeps mumbling about—

THERE was nothing special about the little man who came into Larry's place, unless it might have been his air of vague familiarity and the mixed expression on his face. He looked disgusted and defensive and at the same time a little resentful, with a dash of something else thrown in which none of us recognized until later.

I'd have mistaken him for another reporter from the *Advertiser* across the street if the five newsmen already at the bar hadn't given each other a blank look that meant only one thing: none of them knew him. Neither did Larry, who was trying to bring in the first broadcast from Mars on the television set bracketed to the wall over his whiskey stock, and who wasn't pleased at having his little after-hours party crashed.

"The bar's closed," Larry said. His tone didn't invite argument. "City ordinance. No customers after 1:00 a. m."

The little man looked at the clock, which said 3:15, and then at the front windows which were shuttered tight. Then he looked at the six of us sitting at the bar with our drinks.

"I'll have bourbon and water," he said. He sat down at the end of the bar on the stool next to mine and looked at his reflection in the mirror without approval.

Larry got the look that bartenders get with troublesome customers.

"The bar's closed," he said again. "It's a city—"

"Water on the side," the little man said. "Don't mix it."

Abe Marker, who does sports for the *Advertiser*, got up and checked the front-door lock. The thumb-catch hadn't been thrown, so Abe put it on and came back to the bar.

"Nobody else will wander in," he said. "Make with the tv, Larry. You're holding up the show."

Larry looked stubborn.

"It's after 1:00 a. m.," he said. "And that door was supposed to be locked. There's a city ordinance—"

"You're breaking it already," the little man said, looking at us. He didn't seem angry, just weary and disgusted. "Not that I give a damn. All I want is a bourbon and water."

"Better give it to him, Larry," Willard Saxton said from down the bar. Willard is the *Advertiser's* science editor and is an authority on the planets, especially Mars. "He'll probably turn you in if you throw him out."

Larry muttered and looked mulish, but he rang up the little man's money and gave him a bourbon and water. The little guy drank it and looked at himself in the bar mirror with an expression that was just short of being a sneer. Larry grunted and went back to fiddling with the television set.

Abe Marker came over and sat down on the stool to my left.

"They're doing this all over town tonight," he said, explaining to the little man across me. "The bars have to observe curfew as usual, but most of them are letting a few regular customers stay late to see the Marscast. Everybody is anxious to know what Colonel Sanderson and his crew found up there, so—"

"They're going to be disappointed," the little man said. He sounded sour but positive. "Mars ain't what people think it is, not by a hell of a sight. It stinks."

We all looked up at that, and somebody snickered.

"Have you been to Mars, sir?"

The little man didn't seem to mind when we laughed.

"Maybe," he said, and shoved his shot glass forward. "Another bourbon, bartender."

THE station announcer came on screen then and told us what we already knew, that contact with Colonel Sanderson's party was delayed because of transmission difficulties. The

Sanderson expedition would leave Mars for Earth in two more days, when the current opposition was completed, but in the meantime the program sponsors appreciated the interest shown by their public and would relay the broadcast to us as soon as contact was established.

A film cartoon featuring a lizard named Freddie came on next, and Larry turned down the sound so he could hear orders for refills. The little man drank his bourbon and water and sneered at his reflection in the mirror; none of us paid him any further attention, but talk started up again along the bar.

Somebody at the other end asked how long it took a television signal to travel across all that space, and choked on his drink when Willard Saxton told him.

"My God," he said when he stopped coughing. "You mean Mars is so far away it takes three minutes just to see it?"

All of us laughed at that but Larry and the little man at the end of the bar.

"What I'm wondering," somebody else said, "is how the colonel and his boys feel after breathing nothing but canned air for a year."

"Maybe the air up there is better than our scientists think," Abe Marker said. He winked at us and looked at the little man on my right. "How about it, friend? Is the air good on Mars?"

"Breathable, but not good," the little guy said. "It smells like dead fish."

Silence fell along the bar while we waited for a straight man to raise his head.

Willard Saxton took the bait. "And why should it smell so, may I ask?"

"Because Mars is lousy with fish," the little man said. "And because when fish die, they stink."

Larry did a brisk business for a few minutes while we sized the little guy up again. He definitely wasn't drunk, but the task of deciding whether he was being deadpan-comic or just nasty was a sort of challenge that called for thought.

"But you'd need extensive oceans to support so many fish," Willard Saxton argued, still taking it seriously. "And if Mars had oceans we'd have seen them long ago. They reflect light."

"Mars is too level for oceans," the little man said. "The water spreads out thin to make one big marsh, and you can't see it because the weeds that grow up from the bottom camouflage it."

Somebody down the bar said, "This gets curioser and curioser," and everybody laughed again but Willard and Larry and the little comic. Somebody else asked if he was a professional and what show was he on, but he didn't answer. He just pushed his shot glass forward instead.

"Another bourbon," he said.

The announcer came on screen again when the lizard cartoon went off and said that the Mars party's signal was beginning to come through and that as soon as it cleared up they would put it on the cable. Then he told us about a new kind of pretzel prepared with a special salt guaranteed not to give us hardening of the arteries, and after that we had another film cartoon. This one was about two crows at a circus, but nobody could follow it because Larry turned down the sound again.

Between his third and fourth stingers Willard Saxton—who had a reputation to uphold, being science editor of the *Advertiser*—had made up his mind by now to put the little man in his place. It burned him brown to see this character drinking bourbon and sneering at himself in the mirror and not caring a damn what we thought, and it put Willard under a sort of obligation to show him up.

"Reliable tests have conclusively proved," Willard said, "that the atmosphere of Mars contains only minute traces of water vapor, and that its oxygen content is less than one-hundredth the density necessary to sustain human life. Spectroanalysis findings—"

"A spectroanalysis of Earth from Mars," the little man said, "shows nothing beyond our Heaviside layer, and proves that we can't live here because nothing can breathe pure ozone."

HE finished his bourbon and made chains of wet rings on the bartop with his glass. The mixed look on his face was so strong that for a moment I almost thought of the name for it.

Willard stalled for time by ordering another stinger—a double, this time—and Abe Marker took over.

"How about those pictures of Martian dust storms the boys at Palomar make?" Abe asked. "You can't have dust storms on a marshy planet, can you?"

"Those aren't dust storms," the little man said. "They're clouds of gnats."

"*Gnats?*" we all said at once, and somebody down the bar, quicker-witted than the rest of us, added: "Gnats to you too, Charlie!"

"A fact," the little man said, but not as if he cared. "They travel in swarms thousands of miles wide, and they bite like hell."

We sat and watched the two voiceless crows flap through the television cartoon for a while. Nobody spoke until the film was over and the screen went blank, when the little man caught Larry's eye and held up one finger.

"Bourbon," he said.

We heard a confused muttering of voices in the background and waited expectantly for Colonel Sanderson to speak to us from Mars, but apparently the network people were still having trouble with their transmission beam. The screen stayed blank.

"You left out the interesting part, Charlie," somebody called from down the bar. "The Martian natives. How about them?"

"There aren't any—as you'd know them," the little man said. He seemed to grow thoughtful for a moment. "But they are intelligent. They do things you couldn't do."

"Such as what?" somebody asked.

The little man shrugged. "Teleport. They're good at it too."

Saxton let out a laugh. "That would make them more intelligent than us!" he said. "What do these Martians look like?"

The little man screwed up his face distastefully. "Frogs."

The reporter who had asked about natives got choked on his drink and had to be pounded on the back. On my left, Abe Marker leaned against the bar to look past me at the little guy.

"Frogs we got now," he said admiringly. "By the billions?"

"There are more frogs on Mars," the little man said, "than there are gnats and fish together, and they never stop croaking. You'd have to hear it to believe it."

The television screen lit up suddenly, chopping off conversation, and we were watching the first Marscast in history.

COLONEL Sanderson himself was talking. He looked the way Stanley must have looked when he found Livingstone, gaunt and bearded and jumpy; and his crew, lined up behind him before the ship's pickup camera, were in no better shape. The lot of them stared hungrily out at us as if they had just found a peephole into Heaven and couldn't wait to see if there was a gate farther along the fence.

"...established conceptions of Martian areography are completely erroneous," the colonel was saying. "There are no drifting deserts of sand or howling typhoons of ferrous dust. We can show you actual conditions better by camera, I think, than they could be detailed in words."

The view jumped to another camera aimed from an outside port, and we saw Mars. Colonel Sanderson's voice kept up a running commentary behind the scene, but we only half heard him.

The ship rested in about two feet of water. Around it the whole world curved up to the horizon in a shallow concave sweep like the inside of a great rusty bowl, lined with knee-high reeds that grew as far as the eye could see out of a knee-deep marsh. A fist-sized sun hung low in the sky, its glare dulled to a muddy crimson by a shimmering cloud of gnats that whirled and danced to infinity. There was a sort of vast, featureless roaring in the background that sounded like Niagara at two hundred yards, not deafening but loud enough to force Colonel Sanderson to raise his voice.

"The frog noise is worst," he was saying. "It drives us to the point of insanity at times... One member of our party has succumbed to it already, a machinist named Willkins who disappeared two weeks ago. Apparently the poor fellow drowned himself in the marsh, since no trace of him has been found since."

That was when I realized why the little man on the stool beside me looked so familiar—because I had seen his pictures in the papers, along with the rest of Sanderson's crew, a thousand times during the past year. The mixed expression on his face made sense now, too; he wasn't only disgusted and defensive, he was *guilty*.

"So that's how you knew what it was like," I said, "You couldn't stick it out with the others, so you jumped ship. You deserted!"

He gave me a hangdog look. "It's not deserting unless the country is at war," he said. "It's just going over the hill, A.W.O.L."

The television roar got louder, and when I looked up the ship's cameraman was doing a close-up for our benefit. He panned the shot downward until we seemed to be standing ten feet above the marsh, and at that distance I could see plainly what it was that caused the uproar.

The water between the reddish-brown reeds was thick with huge frogs, all blinking and croaking like mad.

I remember thinking then that you couldn't really blame a man for jumping ship in a hole like that. It was bad enough to be stuck thirty-odd million miles from home, so far that light itself needed three minutes to—

"Hey, wait up!" I said to the little guy, who was sneering at himself in the mirror again. "If you went A.W.O.L. up there, then how the hell did you get back *here?*"

I didn't find out.

The guy was gone. He had been standing there so close I could have touched him, but now he was gone. I looked around quick. Nobody else seemed to have noticed. All eyes were on the TV screen.

Then I saw it. On the floor. Two wet marks—right where the guy should have been, where he *was*. Two wet marks that had a funny shape to them—web-like.

I felt my throat tighten at the thought. I shook my head. What was going through it was fantastic, impossible and downright lunacy. There was an intelligent life-form on Mars— beings that looked like frogs and could teleport. Could they also mimic human shape temporarily? Especially if they got hold of one for a model—say a missing crewman...

"Hey! Where are you going? Don't you want to see the Marscast?"

I was walking to the door. I looked back at the barkeep. "I've seen enough, Larry, I got things to do."

He shrugged. "Yeh, what?"

"Like hunting frogs," I told him as I shoved the door open. "I got a hunch we'll be doing a lot of that before very long..."

THE END

Exiles of Tomorrow

By MARION ZIMMER BRADLEY

Into the brightly youthful fabric of Carey Kennaird's life was woven the dark and hateful tyranny of the world his birth had shattered.

CHAPTER ONE

"A VERY STRANGE thing happened when I was born," Carey Kennaird told me.

He paused and refilled his wineglass, looking at me with a curious appraisal in his young and very blue eyes. I returned his glance as casually as I could, wondering why he had suddenly decided to confide in me.

I had known Carey Kennaird for only a few weeks. We were the most casual of acquaintances; a word in the lobby of our hotel, a cup of coffee in a lunchroom he liked, mugs of beer in the quiet back room of the corner bar. He was intelligent and I had enjoyed his conversation. But until now it had consisted entirely of surface commonplaces. Today, he seemed to be opening up a trifle.

He had volunteered the information, unasked, that he was the son of a well-known research physicist, and that he was in Chicago to look for his father who had disappeared mysteriously a week or so before. Young Kennaird seemed oddly unworried about his father's plight. But I was pleased at the way his reserve appeared to be dropping.

As I say, Carey Kennaird had a casual way with him, and he puzzled me. He did not, somehow, seem emotionally in sympathy with the hectic tempo of the rushed age in which he had grown up.

"Well," I told him noncommittally, "childhood memories often make quite normal events seem strange. What was it?"

The appraisal in his eyes was franker now. "Mr. Grayne, do you ever read science fiction?"

"I'm afraid not," I told him. "At least, only very occasionally."

He looked a little crestfallen.

"Oh—well, do you know anything about the familiar science fiction concept of traveling in time?"

"A little." I finished my drink, wishing the waiter would bring us another bottle of wine. "It's supposed to involve some quite staggering paradoxes, I believe. I'm thinking of the man who goes back in time and kills his own grandfather."

He looked disgusted. "That's at best a trite layman's idea!"

"Well, I'm a layman," I said genially. The arrogance of young people always strikes me as being pathetic rather than insulting. I did not think young Kennaird could have been more than nineteen. Twenty, perhaps. "Now then, young fellow, don't tell me you've actually invented a time machine!"

"Good Lord, no!" The denial was so laughingly spontaneous that I had to laugh with him. "No, just an idea that interests me. I don't really believe there's much paradox involved in time-travel at all."

He paused, his eyes still on my face. "See here, Mr. Grayne, I'd like to—well, do you mind listening to something rather fantastic? I'm not drunk, but I've got a good reason for wanting to confide in you. You see, I know a great deal about you, really."

I wasn't surprised. In fact, I'd been prepared for just such a statement. I grinned a strained grin at the boy. "No, go ahead," I told him. "I'm interested." I leaned back in my chair, preparing to listen.

You see, I knew what he was going to say.

CHAPTER TWO

Ryn Kenner sat in his cell, his head buried in his hands.

"Oh, God—" he muttered to himself, over and over.

There were so many unpredictable risks involved. Even though he had spent three years coaching Cara, teaching her to guard against every possible contingency, he still might fail. If only he could have eliminated the psychic block. But that, of course, was the most necessary risk of all.

Sometimes, in spite of his humanitarian training, Ryn Kenner thought the old, primitive safeguards had been better. Executing murderers, locking maniacs up in cells was certainly better than exiling men in this horrible new way. Ryn Kenner knew that he would have preferred to die. Two or three times he had even thought of slashing his wrists with a razor before the Exile. Once he had actually set a razor against his right wrist, but his early training had been too strong for him. Even the word *suicide* could set off a mental complex of quivering nerve reactions impossible to control.

The tragedy, Kenner thought despondently, resided in the paradox that civilization had become too enlightened. There had been a time when men had thought that traveling backward in time would upset the framework of events and change the future. But it had been a manifestly mistaken idea, for in this year, 2543 A.D., the whole past had already occurred, and the present moment contained within itself the entire past, including whatever rectifying attempts time-travelers had made in that past.

Kenner shivered as he realized that his own acts had all occurred in the past. He, Ryn Kenner, had already died—six centuries before.

Time-travel—the perfect, the most humane way of banishing criminals! He had heard all the arguments which sophistry could muster. The strong individualists were clearly misfits in the enlightened twenty-sixth century. For their own good, they should be exiled to eras psychologically congenial to them. A good many of them had been sent to California in the year 1849. They thus took a one-way trip to an era where murder was not a crime, but a social necessity, the respectable business of a gentleman. Religious fanatics were exiled to the First Dark

Ages, where they could not disturb the tranquil materialism of the present century; too aggressive atheists, to the twenty-third century.

Kenner rose and began to pace his cell, which was a prison in fact, if not in appearance. Outside the wide window spread a spacious view of Nyor Harbor, and the room was luxuriously furnished. He knew however, that if he stepped a foot past the lines which had been drawn around the door, he would be instantly overpowered by a powerful sleeping gas. He had tried it once, with almost disastrous results.

This hour of high decision was his last in the twenty-sixth century. In fifty minutes, in his own personal, subjective time from now, he would be somewhere in the twentieth century, the era to which his rashness had condemned him when he had been apprehended by the psycho police while attempting to re-discover the fabulous atomic isotopes. And he wouldn't remember enough to get back. He would be permitted to keep all his training—all his knowledge, and memory—but there would be a fatal reservation.

Never, for the rest of his life would Kenner be able to remember that he had come from the past. For the three weeks during which he had been confined to the cell the radiant suggestor had been steadily beaming at his brain. No defense his mind could devise had sufficed to stay its slow inroads into his thought.

Already his brain was beginning to grow fuzzy and he knew that the time was short. He drew a long breath, hearing steps in the corridor, and the whistle that meant the hypnotic gas was being momentarily turned off.

He stopped pacing.

Abruptly the door opened, and a psycho-supervisor entered the cell. Framed in the radiance behind him—

"Cara!" Kenner almost sobbed, and ran forward to catch his wife in his arms, and hold her with hungry violence. She cried softly against him. "Rhy, Ryn, it won't be long—"

The supervisor's face was compassionate. "Kenner," he said, "you may have twenty minutes alone with your wife. You will be unsupervised." The door closed softly behind him.

Kenner led Cara to a seat. She tried to hold back her tears, looking at him with wide, frightened eyes. "Ryn, darling, I thought you might have—"

"Hush, Cara," he whispered. "They may be listening. Just remember everything I've told you. You *mustn't* risk being sent to a different year. You already know what to do."

"I'll—find you," she promised.

"Let's not talk about it," Kenner urged gently. "We haven't long. Grayne promised he'd look after you until—"

"I know. He's been good to me while you were here."

The twenty minutes didn't seem long. The supervisor pretended not to notice while Cara clung to Kenner in a last agony of farewell. Ryn brushed the tears away from her eyes, softly.

"See you in nineteen forty-five, Cara," he whispered, and let her go.

"It's a date darling," were her last words before she followed the supervisor out of the prison. Kenner, in the last few moments remaining to him, before he sank into sleep again, desperately tried to marshal what little knowledge he possessed about the twentieth century.

His brain felt dark now, and oppressed, as if someone had wrapped his mind in smothering folds of wool. Dimly he knew that when he woke, his prison would be yet un-built. And yet, all the rest of his life he would be in prison—the prison of a mind that would never let him speak the truth.

CHAPTER THREE

"—and of course, this hypothetical psychic block would also contain provision prohibiting marriage with anyone from the past," Carey Kennaird finished. "It would naturally be inconvenient for children to be born of the time exiles. But if my hypothetical man from the future should actually find the wife he'd arranged to have exiled with him, there'd be no psychic block against marrying *her*." He paused, staring at me steadily. "Now, what would happen to the kid?"

My own glass stood empty. I signaled to the waiter, but Kennaird shook his head. "Thanks, I've had enough."

I paid for the wine. "Suppose we walk to the hotel together, Kennaird?" I said. "You've got a fascinating theory there, my boy. It would make a fine plot for a science fiction novel. Are you a writer? Of course, what happened to the boy—" we passed together into the blinding sunlight of the Chicago Loop, "—would be the climax of your story."

"It would," Kennaird agreed.

We crossed the street beneath the thundering El trains, and stood in front of Marshall Fields while Carey lit a cigarette.

"Smoke?" he asked.

I shook my head. "No thanks. You said you had a reason for confiding in me, young man. What is it?"

He looked at me curiously. "I think you know, Mr. Grayne. You weren't born in the Twentieth Century. I was, of course. But you're like Dad and Cara. You're a time exile, too, aren't you?

"I know you can't *say* anything, because of the psychic block. But you don't have to deny it. That's how Dad told me. He made me read science fiction. Then he made me ask him leading questions—and just answered yes or no." Young Kennaird paused. "I don't have the psychic block. Dad was trying to help me discover the time-travel device. He came up to Chicago, and disappeared. But I'm on the right track now. I'm sure of it. I think Dad got back somehow."

Even though I'd known what he was going to say, I swallowed hard.

"Something very strange *did* happen when you were born," I said. "You put a peculiar strain on the whole framework of time. It was something that never should have happened, because of—" my voice faltered, "the psychic block against marrying anyone from the past."

Carey Kennaird looked at me intently. "Hard to talk about the psychic block, isn't it? Dad never could."

I nodded without speaking. We climbed the hotel steps together. "Come up to my room," I urged. "We'll talk it over. You see, Carey—I'm going to call you that—Kenner used to be my friend."

"I wonder," Carey said, "if dad got home to the twenty-sixth century."

"He did."

Carey stared. "Mr. Grayne! Is he all right?"

Regretfully, I shook my head. The elevator boy let us off on the fourth floor. I wondered if he, too, were an exile. I wondered how many people in Chicago were exiles, sullen behind the mask of a mental block, which damped a gag on their lips when they tried to speak the truth.

I wondered how many men, and how many women, were living such a lie, day in, and day out, lonely, miserable exiles from their own tomorrow, victims of a fate literally worse than death. Small wonder they would do *anything* to avoid such a fate.

My door closed behind us. While Carey stared, wide-eyed, at the device, which loomed darkly in one corner of the room, I went to my desk, and removed the shining disk. I walked straight up to him. "This is from your father," I told him. "Look at it carefully."

He accepted it eagerly, his eyes blazing with excitement, sensing at once that it had come from the twenty-sixth century.

He died instantly.

Hating my work, hating time-travel, hating the whole chain of events, which had made me an instrument of justice, I stepped into the device that would return me to the twenty-sixth century.

Carey Kennaird had told the truth. A very strange thing *had* happened at his birth. Like an extra electron bombarding an unstable isotope, he had broken the link that held the framework of time together. His birth had started a chain reaction that had ended, for me, a week before in 2556, when Kenner and Cara had reappeared in the twenty-sixth century and been murdered in a panic by the psycho-supervisors. I, already condemned to time exile, had won a free pardon for my work, a commutation of my sentence to a light reprimand and the loss of my position. It was ugly work and I hated it, for Kenner and Cara *had* been my friends. But I had no freedom of choice. Anything was better than exile into time.

Anything, anything.

Besides, it had been necessary.

It isn't lawful for children to be born before their parents.

THE END

Half Around Pluto

By MANLY WADE WELLMAN

*Pluto was a coffin world, airless, utterly cold. And they had ten days to
reach Base Camp, ten thousand miles away.*

THEIR glassite space helmets fogged, and their metal glove
joints stiffened in the incredible surface cold; but the two men
who could work finished their job. In the black sky glistered the
little arclight of the sun, a sixteen-hundredth of the blaze that
fell on Earth. Around them sulked Pluto's crags and gullies,
sheathed with the hard-frozen pallor that had been Pluto's
atmosphere, eons ago.

From the wrecked cylinder of the scout rocket they had
dragged two interior girders, ready-curved at the ends. These,
clamped side by side with transverse brackets and decked with
bulkhead metal, managed to look like a sled.

At the rear they set a salvaged engine unit. For steering, they
rigged a boom shaft to warp the runners right or left. For cargo,
they piled the sled with full containers, ration boxes, the foil
tent, what instruments they could detach and carry, armfuls of
heat-tools, a crowbar, a hatchet, a few other items.

Moving back from the finished work, one of them stumbled
against the other. Instantly the two puffy soot-black shapes
were crouched, gloved fists up, fierce in the system's duskiest
corner.

Then the moment passed. Warily, helmets turned toward
each other, they went back to the half-stripped wreck.

In the still airtight control room, lighted by one bulb, their
officer stirred on his bedstrip. His tunic had been pulled off, his
broken left arm and collarbone set and splinted. Under a fillet

of bandage, his gaunt young face looked pale, but he had his wits back.

"The appropriate question," he said, "is 'What happened?'"

The two men were removing their helmets. "Conked and crashed, sir," said Jenks, the smaller one, uncovering a sallow, hollow-cheeked face.

Lieutenant Wofforth sat up, supporting himself on his sound arm. "How long have I been out?"

"Maybe forty hours, sir. Delirious. Corbett and me did the best we could. Take it easy, sir," he said as Wofforth began to get up. "Lie back. We've done what Emergency Plan Six says—bolted a sled together and coupled on a sound engine unit for power."

"Quite a haul back to base," said Wofforth, almost cheerfully. His eyes were bright, as though he savored the idea. "About halfway around Pluto. We'd better start now, or they'll get tired of waiting."

"They've gone, sir," Corbett growled before Jenks could gesture him to silence. He was beefy, slit-eyed. "We saw the jets going sunward this morning."

Wofforth winced. "Gone," he said. "That's right, I didn't stop to think. You said forty hours... They couldn't wait that long. We're past opposition already, getting farther away all the time. They had to go, or they wouldn't have made it."

He stood up uncertainly and reached for his ripped tunic. Corbett stepped over and helped him slide his uninjured arm into the right sleeve, then to fasten and drape the tunic over his splinted left arm and shoulder.

"We'll just have to get back to Base Camp and wait," said Wofforth, grimly.

"Sir," said Jenks, "our radio is gone. I tried to patch it up, but it was gone. When they didn't get a signal, they must have thought—"

"Nonsense!" Wofforth broke in. "They'll have left us supplies. They couldn't wait, signal or none. Our job is to get back, and stick it out there until they come for us."

He sat at the control and began to write in the logbook. Corbett and Jenks drifted together at the other end of the room.

"You meat-head," snarled Jenks under his breath. "You knew he took the berth to Pluto because the first mate was a lady—Lya Stromminger."

"He had to know they were gone," protested Corbett, equally fierce.

"Not flat like you gave it. He came here to be with her. Now she's jetted away without him. How does a man feel when a woman's done that—"

"Stop blathering, you two, and help me into my suit," called Wofforth, rising again. "We're going to rev up that sled engine and get out of here!"

Outside, the sled lay ready under the frigid sky. Wofforth tramped around it, leaned over and poked the load.

"Too much," said his voice in their radios. "Keep the synthesizer, the tent, these two ration boxes. Wait, keep the crowbar and the hatchet. Dump the rest."

"We travel that light, sir?" said Jenks doubtfully.

"I've been figuring," said Wofforth. "We're on the far side of Pluto from Base Camp. That makes ten thousand miles, more or less. Pluto's day is nineteen hours and a minute or so, Earth time. We can travel only by what they humorously call daylight. And we'd better get there in ten days—a thousand miles every nine and a half hours—or maybe we won't get there at all."

"How's that, sir?" asked Corbett.

"The heaters in these suits," Wofforth reminded him. "Two hundred and forty hours of efficiency, and that's all. Well, it's noon. Let's take off."

His voice shook. He was still weak. Jenks helped him sit on the two lashed ration boxes, and slung a mooring strap across his knees. Then Jenks took the steering boom and Corbett bent to start the engine.

When the arclight sunset in the west, they had traveled more than four hours over country not too rugged to slow them much. Darkness closed in fast while Jenks and Corbett pitched the pyramidal tent of metal foil and clamped it down solidly. They spread and zipped in the ground fabric, set up lights and heater inside, and began to pipe in thawed gases from the drifts outside.

After their scanty meal, Corbett and Jenks sought their bedstrips, on opposite sides of the tent. Wofforth tended the atomic heater for minutes, until the sound of deep breathing told him that his companions were asleep.

Then he put on his spacesuit, clumsy with his single hand to close seams. He picked up sextant and telescope, and slipped out into the Plutonian night.

It was as utterly black as the bottom of a pond of ink. But above Wofforth shone the faithful stars, in the constellations mapped by the first stargazers of long ago. He made observations, checked for time and position. He chuckled inside his helmet, as though congratulating himself. Back in the tent, he opened the logbook and wrote:

First day: Course due west. Run 410 mi. To go 9590 mi. approx. Supplies adeq. Spirits good.

Wriggling out of his space gear, he lay down, asleep almost before his weary limbs relaxed.

EVERYONE was awake before dawn. They made coffee on the heater, and broke out protein biscuits for breakfast.

As the tiny sun winked into view over the horizon, they loaded the sled. Corbett slouched toward the idling engine at the tail of the sled.

"No, get on amidships," said Wofforth. "I'll take over engine."

"My job—" began Corbett.

"You're relieved. Strap yourself on the ration boxes. That's right. Jenks, steer again. Make for the level ahead."

With his right hand Wofforth ran a length of pliable cable around his waist and through a ringbolt on the decking. He touched the engine controls, and they pulled away from camp.

The sled coursed over great knoll-like swellings of the terrain, coated with the dull-pale frozen atmosphere. Beyond, it gained speed on a vast flat plain, almost as smooth as a desert of glass.

"What's this big rink, Lieutenant?" asked Jenks.

"Maybe a sea, or maybe just a sunken area, full of solid gases. Stand by the helm, I'm going to gun a few more M. P. H. out of her."

"No wind," grunted Corbett. "Nothing moving except us. The floor of hell."

"If you was in hell, the rest of us would be better off," said Jenks sourly.

Wofforth began to sing, though he did not feel like it:

Trim your nails and scrape your face,
They're all on the Other Side of space!
Tokyo—Baltimore, Maryland—Hong Kong—Paris—Samarkand—
Tokyo—London—Troy—Fort Worth—
The happy towns of the Planet Earth...

At camp that night he wrote in the logbook:

Second Day: Course due west. Run 1014 mi. To go 8576 mi. approx. Supplies adeq. Spirits fair...

"What's for supper?" bawled Corbett, entering. "I could eat a horse."

"That'd be cannibalism," said Jenks at once.

"Yah, you splinter! Don't eat any lizards, then."

Spirits good, Wofforth corrected his entry, and closed the logbook. He thought of Lya Stromminger. She was a most efficient officer. Her hair was black as night on Pluto and her eyes as bright as the faraway sun.

Wofforth wrote in his logbook:

Fifth day: Course north, west, then southwest. Curving thru mountainous territory. Run 1066 mi. but direct progress toward base camp not exceeding 950. To go, 6260 mi. approx. Supplies short. Spirits fair.

He wrote in his logbook:

Seventh day: Course west, southwest, west, northwest, west. Run 1108 mi. To go 4090 mi. approx. Supplies low. Spirits fair.

He wrote in his logbook:

Ninth day: Course northwest by west, west. Run 1108 mi. To go 2030 mi. approx. Supplies low. Spirits low...

"Lieutenant," said Jenks from across the tent, as Wofforth closed the book.

"Well?"

"We know you're in command. This party and all of Pluto. But we ask permission to state our case."

"What case is your case?" demanded Wofforth, rising. "I'm doing my best to get you back to Base Camp."

"Sure," said Corbett. "Sure. But why Base Camp?"

"You know why."

"That's right, we know why," agreed Jenks, and Corbett grinned in his ten days' tussock of beard.

"They'll have left supplies for us," Wofforth went on. "Shelter and food and fuel and instruments. They'll expect us to reach Base Camp and hold it down for the next attempt to reach Pluto."

"We know why," repeated Jenks. "And that's not why, lieutenant. Let me talk, sir. It's a dead man talking."

"You won't die," snapped Wofforth. "I'll get you both there alive."

He stepped to where, in one corner, he had managed a bath—a hollow in the frozen ground, lined by pushing the floor fabric into it. From the heater he ran tepid, clean water into it. He clipped a mirror to the tent foil, searched out an automatic razor, and began to shave his own dark young thatch of beard.

"You're proving my point, lieutenant," said Jenks. "Policing up your face to look pretty."

"Why not?" growled Wofforth, mowing another swath of whiskers.

"No reason why not. Ten, twenty years from now they'll find your body—whenever the inner orbits get to where they can boom off another expedition. You'll look young and clean-shaved. You know who'll weep."

Wofforth lowered the razor in his good hand and glared at the two. They grinned in the bright light opposite him. They looked as if they hoped he'd see the joke.

"I said it's a dying man that's talking," said Jenks again. "Won't you let me say my dying say, lieutenant? Let's all die honest."

"I'm going to get you there," Wofforth insisted.

"Ah, now," said Corbett, as though persuading a naughty child. "You think they've left twenty years' worth of supplies to keep us going? The ship didn't carry that much, even if they left it all," he grinned mirthlessly. "I can figure what you're figuring, lieutenant," he went on, with a touch of Jenks' sly manner. "You die, young and brave. You'll shave up again before you lie down and let go. And when the next shipload arrives there'll be you, lying like a statue of your good-looking young self, frozen stiff. Am I right?"

Corbett was right, Wofforth admitted to himself. The man was more than a great meaty lump, after all, to see another man's unspoken thought so clearly.

"Then," Jenks took it up, "First Mate Lya Stromminger will have a look. She may command the new expedition. She'll be promoted away up to Admiral or higher—twenty years of brilliant service—gone gray around the edges, but still a lovely lady. There you'll lie before her eyes, young and brave as you was when she deserted you. She'll cry, won't she? And hot tears can't thaw you out or wake you up—"

"Shut your heads, both of you!" shouted Wofforth, so fierce and loud that the foil tent wall vibrated as with a gale in the airless night.

But they had guessed true. He'd wanted to be found at Base Camp. He'd wanted Lya Stromminger to know, some day, that she'd blasted off and left behind the man most worthy of all men on all worlds...

"Everybody takes a hot bath tonight," said Wofforth. "We'll all sleep better for it. Tomorrow's our last day on the trail."

"To do two thousand miles?" said Jenks.

"To do all of that. The expedition mapped an area at least that wide around Base Camp, and it's slick and smooth. We can almost slide in."

"All slick and smooth but just this side of Base Camp, lieutenant," said Jenks.

"How do you mean?"

"That string of craters. Don't you remember? It's just this side east of Base Camp. This sled'll never go over that, sir."

"Nor around," Corbett put in. "We'd have to detour maybe three thousand miles. And the heaters in our suits won't last."

"I know about the craters," said Wofforth. "We'll take care of them when we reach them."

Stripping, he lowered his body into the makeshift tub and began to scrub himself one-handed.

HE WAKENED in the morning to the sound of furious argument.

Corbett and Jenks, of course. A trifle-division of the breakfast ration, or of the breakfast chores had set off their nerves like trains of explosive. Even as Wofforth rose from his bedstrip, Corbett swung a cobble-like fist at Jenks' gaunt, grimacing face. The nimbler, smaller man ducked and sidled away. Corbett took a lumbering step to close in on his enemy, and Jenks darted a hand to his belt behind, then brought it forward again with an electro-automatic pistol.

"I've been keeping this for you!" Jenks shrilled. "I'll just diminish the population of Pluto by thirty-three and one-third percent!"

"Hold it!" bellowed Wofforth.

He was too late. A stream of bullets chattered through Corbett's body, folding him over and ripping through the paper-thin wall of the tent. Air whistled out; the tent began to collapse.

Jenks, pinned under Corbett's body, was squealing like a pig. "Lieutenant, help me—!"

Wofforth saw in an instant that the wall could not be patched in time; the bullets had torn loose an irregular strip, pressure had done the rest: even now, the tent was only a few seconds away from complete collapse. As he stumbled across the floor toward the spacesuits, his heart was laboring and his chest straining for breath. Spots swam in front of his eyes. He found the topmost spacesuit by touch, and fumbled for the helmet. The tent drifted down on his head in soft, murderous folds. He opened the valve, shoved his face into the helmet, and gulped precious oxygen. His dulled awareness brightened again, momentarily; but he knew he was still a dead man unless he could get into the suit before pressure fell completely. Numbed fingers plucked at the suit opening. Somehow he got the awkward garment over his legs, closed and locked the torso, pulled down the helmet...

He was lying in darkness, with a low, steady hiss of oxygen in his ears. He rolled over weakly, got to his feet. He turned on his helmet light. He was propping up a gray cave of metal foil that fell in stiff creases all around him. At his feet were the bodies of Jenks and Corbett. Both were dead.

After a while, clumsily, painfully, he dragged the two corpses free of the tent. He found the heater and thawed a hole in the frozen surface, big enough for both. He tumbled them in, then undercut the edges of the hole with the heater, so that chunks fell in and covered them. While he watched, the cloud of vapor he had made began to settle, slowly congealing on the broken surface and blurring it over again. In a year, there would be no mark here to show that the surface had been disturbed. In a thousand years, it would still be the same.

In the first ray of dawn he flung all supplies from the sled except the fuel containers. He checked the engine, and started it.

Into his belt-bag he thrust the logbook. Nothing else went aboard the sled—no food, no water container, no tools, instruments or oxygen tanks. The tent he left lying there, with all that had been carried inside the night before.

As the sun rose clear of the distant rim of the plain to eastward, he rigged a line to the steering boom, then lashed himself securely within reach of the engine. Steering by the taut line, he started westward, slowly at first, then faster. It was as he had hoped. The lightened sled attained and held a greater speed than on any previous day.

"I'll make it," he said aloud, with nobody else to listen on all Pluto. "I'll make it!"

Faster he urged the engine's rhythm, and faster. He clocked its speed by the indicators on the housing. A hundred and fifty miles an hour. A hundred and sixty; not enough. Whipping the boom line tight around his waist to hold his course steady, he sighted between the upcurve of the runner forward. There was level, smooth-frozen country, mile upon mile. He speeded up to one hundred and seventy-five miles an hour. More. The sled hummed at every joining.

At noon, he had done a good thousand miles. At mid-afternoon, sixteen hundred. Two and a half hour's of visibility left, and more than four hundred miles to go.

"I can do those on my head," muttered Wofforth to himself, and then, far in the distance, the flat rim of the horizon was flat no longer.

It had sprung up jagged, full of points and bulges. Speeding toward it, he steered by the line around his waist while he cut his engine. He came close at fifty miles an hour, almost a crawl.

Some ancient volcanic action had thrown up those mountains, like a rank of close-drawn sentries. The sled could not cross them anywhere. Still reducing speed, Wofforth drew close to a notch, but the notch gave into a crater, a great shallow saucer two miles in diameter and filled with shadows below, so that Wofforth could not gauge its depth. Opposite, another notch—perhaps once the crater had been a lake, with water running in and out. If he had come there at noon, he could have seen the bottom, and perhaps—

"But it isn't noon." Wofforth was talking to himself again. His voice sounded thin and petulant in his own ears. "By noon tomorrow, the heat will be out of this suit."

He stopped the sled, unlashed himself and trudged to the notch. He stood in it, looking down, then across.

The little bright jewel of the sun, sagging toward the horizon, showed him the upper reaches of the crater's interior, pitched at an angle of perhaps fifty degrees.

Even if it had been noon, it would have been no use. The sled could never climb a slope like that.

Then he looked again, this way and that. He nodded inside his helmet.

He might as well try.

Returning to the sled, he started the engine and lashed himself fast again. He steered away from the crater, and around. He made a great looping journey of twenty miles or so across the plain, building speed all the time.

As he rounded the rear curve of his course, he was driving along at two hundred and sixty miles an hour, and he had to apply pressure to the boom with both hand and knees to point the sled back straight for the notch. Straightening his humming vehicle into a headlong course, he leaned forward and sighted between the upcurved runners.

"Now!" he urged himself, and watched the break in the crater wall rush toward him.

It greatened, yawned. He leaped through, and with a groaning gasp of prayer he dragged the boom over to steer the sled right.

IT WORKED, as he had not dared hope. The runners bounced, bit. Then he was racing around the inside of the great cup's rim, like a hurtling bubble on the inner surface of a whirlpool's funnel. Two miles across, three miles and more on the half diameter—the engine laboring up to three hundred miles an hour, centrifugal force holding it there—

Little more than thirty seconds raced by when he knew he had won. He saw the far notch growing near. He came to it in a last booming rush, and hurled his whole weight against the boom to face the runners into the notch.

Under the low-dropping sun, he and his sled shot into open country beyond the range.

His right arm felt dead from shoulder to fingertip. His head roared and drummed with the racing of his blood. His face had tired spots in it, where muscles he had never used before had locked into an agonized grimace.

On he sped, straight west, gasping and gurgling and mumbling in crazy triumph.

An hour, an anticlimactic hour wherein the sled almost steered itself over the smoothest of plain, and up ahead he spied the black outline of Base Camp.

It was a sprawling, low structure, prefabricated metal and plastic and insulation, black outside to gather what heat might come from outer space. It held aloof on the dull frozen plain from the irregular stain where the expedition ship had braked off with one set of rockets and had soared away with another set. Larger, more familiar, grew Base Camp with each second of approach. Shakily Wofforth cut his engine, slowed from high speed to medium, to a hundred miles an hour, to sixty, to fifty. He made a final circle around Base Camp, and let it coast in with the engine off, to within twenty yards of the main lock panel.

He got up, on legs that shook inside his boots. He felt his heart still racing, his head still ringing. He sighed once, and walked close, his gauntlet fumbling at the release button on the lock panel.

But the button did not respond. "Jammed," he said. "No— locked."

He couldn't get in. He had reached Base Camp, but he could not get in. They hadn't counted on his return. They'd gone off and left Base Camp locked up.

He sagged against the lock panel, and cursed once, with an utter and furious resignation.

He felt himself slipping. He was going to faint. His legs would not hold him up. He was slipping forward—seemed to be sinking into the massive and unyielding outer surface of Base Camp. It was a dream. Or it was death.

He did not lose all hold on his awareness. He had a sense of lying at full length, and blinding light flashes that made his eyelids jump. And a tug somewhere, as though his helmet was coming off. He would have put out a hand to see, but his left arm was broken, and his right arm limp from weariness.

"You're back," said a voice he knew, a voice strained with wonder. "You managed. I knew you would."

"Now," said Wofforth, "I know it's a dream. We dream after we die."

A hand was cupped behind his neck, lifting him to a sitting position. He felt warm fluid at his lips. "It's no dream," said the voice beseechingly. "Look at me."

"I don't dare. The dream will go away."

But he opened his eyes and looked at her hair like Plutonian night, her eyes like bright stars. "Lya," he said. "I'm going to call you Lya."

"Please call me Lya."

"I'd be bound to dream about you. I've dreamed about you so much...*Owww!*"

He got his right hand up to cherish his tingling cheek.

"So you felt that," she said. "Now you know you're awake. Or must I slap you again?"

"I'm sorry, Madame."

"You called me Lya. Can you stand up? I'll help you."

She helped him. He stood up, there in the admission chamber of Base Camp. Lya Stromminger was smiling, and she was crying, too.

"You didn't go away," he said. "You're still here." The weight of his odyssey, half around Pluto, was beginning to stagger him.

"No, I stayed. I knew you'd come back. I knew Pluto couldn't kill you or keep you from coming back."

He drank more from the cup she held to his lips.

"We'll wait together for them to come with the next expedition," she promised him.

"Twenty years? Supplies—"

"There'll be plenty. Don't you know about Pluto? Didn't those craters, those old volcanoes, tell you?"

Thinking of how he had crossed the crater, Wofforth shuddered.

"Pluto is colder than anybody even guessed—outside. But inside are the internal fires—like all the solid planets. We made our tests and we can tap them. I kept the instruments for that. It means we'll have power, and can make our synthetic foods and so on for as long as we need them. You are I are the inhabitants here—"

He stumbled to a chair and sat. "Twenty years—" he said.

Her arm was still around him. Her hair brushed his cheek. "It won't be long. We have so much to say to each other."

THE END

Never Gut-shoot a Wampus

By WINSTON MARKS

An interstellar hunting trip with Major Daphne could teach a man a number of lessons. Like being kind to fellow human beings, or—

I'M not exactly broke, but this Major Daphne owned more planets than I do golf balls. Whereas my mining interests were mostly on earth, the Major got in early on the Centaurus grab. A whole generation later, all I could stake out was one hot little hunk of tropical mud that no one else would fool with.

Daphne liked to kid me about my "galactic empire" every time we collided at the club. I was a bachelor and Daphne was married, but he spent more time there than I.

He was a bear of a man with a bull-moose voice, the chest and shoulders of an ape, the appetite of a goat and the morals of a rabbit. There were few wealthier men in the system and none half so noisy about it. His favorite approach to bragging was to tell of his interstellar hunting expeditions.

It costs money to push even a private boat around out there, and nobody but a fatheaded, ostentatious trillionaire would consider blowing half a billion to shoot a brace of pink-eyed grouse, or travel a parsec to blast a two-ton Lartizian lizzard.

He nailed me one morning in the slime-bath at the club. I was soaking out a hangover and a few wrinkles in the filthy antibiotic goo up in health service, when Major Daphne charged in with a towel around his fat middle and plunked down in the next vat. He splashed a gob of the vile smelling green stuff in my face, and I cursed him out.

He bristled at me as he settled his bulk on the sunken stool, "Young man," he growled, "profanity is the luxury of uneducated lackeys and foul-mouthed jackals. Which are you?"

"Splash me again and I'll come over and drown you in this snot," I told him.

He squinted under his gray eyebrows and roared, "Oho! It's my empire-builder friend! Say, when are we going hunting on that free-floating pimple of yours?"

When are *we* going hunting! He had never so much as bought me a drink, and all of a sudden we were buddy-buddies, "What's the matter?" I said, "run out of game on your private preserves?"

"Just looking for amusement, my boy, I've put a hole in a dozen of every specie on 17 planets. Covered all my Centaurus holdings, but never did get around to, to—what do you call that little spitwad of yours?"

He sounded serious, and an idea popped into my head. "That little spitwad is Tigursh II, and it happens to be the hottest big animal planet in the system."

"Sounds gamey," he nodded. "Have you looked around it much?"

I had made only one trip to drop off a prospecting party on the north polar plains. That was two years ago, and all the word I'd had since was a couple of double-talking messages relayed from Centaurii III, asking either double wages or immediate pickup and dismissal for the whole party.

Sometime in the near future I must get out there and investigate personally, but I had been stalling the trip to accumulate the liquid assets it took to lease a ship and outfit from the main base on Centaurii III.

"Been all over it," I lied. "It's not much for comfort, but it's hell for targets. Some really big stuff out there." This last was true. In the week I had spent on the edge of the grassy plateau I had seen a number of herds of heavy-bodied four-leggers galumphing about.

"We'll make up a little party," the Major decided. "Get yourself and your friends out to Centaurii III, and I'll provide a small craft and the gear for the hop over to, to—what did you call it?"

"Tigursh II," I told him happily. This was what I had hoped. The $80,000 passage out to the system I could afford, and with Daphne footing the rest of the bill I would save myself quite a piece of change.

"How many will be in your party?" he wanted to know. "I'll send word ahead for suitable accommodations and supplies."

"I hunt light," I told him. "There'll be just me."

"Hmm. You must be nuts about the sport. You don't mind if I bring along a little diversion?"

"It's your party," I reminded him, more to confirm that he was expected to foot the bills than just to be agreeable.

"I'll keep my party small, too," he promised. "Just the wife and—a few nieces."

THE Major and his party were already gassed and crated when I arrived at the space-deck for the big jump, so it wasn't until they pulled the needle out of me on Daphne's planet at main base that I got a look at his wife and *nieces*.

From that moment until we put down on Tigursh II, the shuttle trip was one continuous party. Beside Daphne, there were Annellica, his legal wife, and six variously hued, large-breasted, slender-hipped young women, each of different planetary origin and talents.

When we were gathered in the cushion-lined salon of the Major's "cosy", 200-foot hunting craft, he introduced them in two sections.

"My wife, Annellica," he said with a casual bow in her direction, "and my nieces." His face brightened with pleasure as he regarded them tumbled around on the billowing underfoot. Although their costumes were of different colors they were all of singularly identical design. They wore one-piece dresses, demurely high-necked, puffed at the shoulders, belted at the narrow waists—and that was all. The flounced skirts stood out as if heavily starched, but they rippled and floated in the diminished gravity with a most titivating effect.

Annellica wore pants.

I said I was charmed, but actually I was appalled, especially when the Major explained. "I only brought along six nieces this trip. Three for you and three for me."

Where, I wondered, did this leave Annellica? The ship lifted under us without warning, and we tumbled about in a gay tangle of giggles and heavy perfume—all but Annellica and me. We were thrown together, and we lay on our sides motionless, nose to nose, staring into each other's eyes.

"Hello," I said. She heaved herself up against the two-gee pressure and leaned on an elbow regarding me with quiet, gray eyes. Her skin was white, but it was still a relief when she answered in unaccented Aminglish.

"Hello!" she answered. "Thank heavens you speak earth."

At our feet Daphne was tumbling up his galactic geishas with lusty shouts of laughter and gabbling in six different dialects.

"Are you a linguist?" she asked. I shook my head, and she smiled for the first time. "Good!" she exclaimed. "You'll get tired of that bird-talk and pay some attention to me."

She sold herself short. Conversational boredom was the least likely reason I would seek the company of this fabulous creature. Daphne was completely engrossed with two wriggling, giggling extra-terrestrials at the moment, so I rolled back and took in the rest of my hostess with an indiscreet survey.

In gray slacks and high-neck T-shirt, she presented the ever pleasantly mysterious enticement of the fully clothed female. Already my interest in the nieces and their leggy displays faded in favor of the one possibly forbidden morsel aboard.

I reached out to touch the unbelievable platinum hair, but she frowned a warning. "Look, but don't touch," she said softly. I misunderstood, but Daphne put me right on the subject. He was looking over at us.

"You're wasting your time," he called. "She's colder than a methane popsicle. A real chip off of Jupiter. Let's eat, whadda ya say? Come, Nelly, produce!"

Annellica sighed. "That belly of his! Life is one continuous smorgasbord. Excuse me, Mr. Frost." She arose cautiously against the double gravity, but even under these circumstances not a line of her firm curves drooped excessively. She was, I guessed, early thirtyish, judging from her mature manner, but she was firm and resilient as a girl of 18.

THE nieces had tired of scuffling in the heavier pull of out acceleration and lay with their cunning costumes plastered to their limp, moist bodies. The Major tried a few last tickles, but the responses were unsatisfactory grunts of fatigue.

He hauled himself over to me.

"Great girl, that Nellie. She's my gun-bearer. By the way, what weapons do you use?"

"Whatever you brought along," I said. "This is your show."

"Good, good! They ought to outlaw these nasty little nuclear side arms. No sport at all. I'm a powder and lead man, myself. Give me a good rifle any day. Primitive but positive, if you know what you're doing."

In amazement I asked, "You use inert projectiles on unknown game?"

"Certainly. Oh, I've had a few close ones, but I learned my lesson in Africa. I got over my impulse to gut-shoot everything that ran at me." He showed me a wrinkled red scar on one shoulder at the base of his bull-neck. "You never want to gut-shoot a lion. He keeps coming. Lead has plenty of impact, but it mushes up and loses its shocking effect in the entrails. You got to break a bone to be sure on these fast beasties. Same thing's true with most of these Wampuses."

"Wampuses?" I asked.

"It's what I call any fast moving game that wears its skeleton on the inside," he explained. "Some on every planet. Carnivorous. Teeth, claws and a hell of an appetite's about all they have in common. Come in all shapes, but main thing is they come at you fast. A lion covers a hundred yards in a little more than three seconds. Some of these extra-t's do better than that."

I tried to look casual, but the truth was that I had never fired at a living target in my life.

"Never gut-shoot a wampus," he repeated. "Break a bone. That gives you time to finish him off."

Our sanguinary conversation ended with the appearance of a circular tray loaded with food. It slid in silently, supported from a silvery, over-head trestle. When it reached us it lowered to the pillowed deck, and the Major fell to with both hands.

He had eaten only a few bites when the uncomfortable plummeting of the food down his gullet reminded him of the heavy pull of acceleration. He threw back his head and roared into the concealed microphone over-head, "Ease off to one gee, captain. A man can't enjoy his food."

After a brief pause a man's voice answered, "We'll have to re--plot the orbit, and it will cost us several days at lower acceleration, Major."

"Ease off while we eat, then pick it up again," Daphne snapped, oblivious to the work he was creating for the navigator. "And don't make me heave when you do it, either!"

The pressure gradually diminished to normal earth gravity. Daphne belched with relief. "That's better."

Annellica was back. She and the girls joined Daphne, nibbling at the platters of meats and swallowing copious quantities of a golden, low-alcohol fluid they sucked from collapsible containers.

"Better eat, Frost," Daphne insisted. "Be in free flight for a bit, and you want to keep up your strength. I can't eat well in free flight. Makes me gassy."

I forced down a few mouthfuls of the exotic rations, wondering why a steward hadn't served us instead of Annellica. After the meal the girls began to perform for us—three of them, singing, dancing and producing weird music on tiny instruments they inserted in their mouths. The other three, Daphne told me, were strictly free flight artists from low gee planets.

Annellica watched for a few minutes then got up and followed the food tray as it drifted away from us. I went after her. In the galley I found her stowing the remnants back into refrigeration. She didn't wait for me to ask the question.

"Daffy dislikes personal servants," she said. "Roboid servers are not practical on the smaller craft, so I take care of our wants."

SHE scraped some half-chewed food into a disposal unit and slipped the plate into a slot: the wife of the wealthy Major Daphne, handling garbage! Cook and gun-bearer!

"You must love him very much," I said.

"Love?" She turned to face me. "What has love to do with—anything?" That was cue enough for me.

I couldn't convince myself she was as frigid as the Major asserted. And I was right. She came into my arms like a hungry tigress. After the most interesting moment of its kind in my eventful bachelorhood, she peeled herself away and went back to her chores.

I gasped, "Lady! What your husband doesn't know about you!"

"And he'll never find out," she said instantly. "He only holds precious things he can't have. My love—passion—call it what you will, is one thing he can't buy."

"I'm afraid I don't understand," I said. "Why did you marry him if—"

"It was that or die a spinster. Every young man who looked twice at me disappeared. At first I thought Daffy would get tired of being married to a perennial virgin, but I was wrong. It's the only thing that has kept him interested in me."

I said, "I suppose it's a natural form of perversity for a man of his wealth and power."

She wheeled, hands on hips. "Perverse? Yes, he's perverse. And perverted and bestial and greedy, boorish, cruel, inhuman, self-centered, insane, piggish—"

She glanced over my shoulder and stopped. "And a completely devoted husband," Major Daphne slobbered behind me. He reeled through the entry, loose-lipped, disheveled and very drunk. He brushed me aside and lurched past me, arms outstretched. "My li'l Nellie's only one 'preciates me."

For a second Annellica was a platinum-haired statue, then she moved to meet him, bringing up an expert knee that struck too high to injure him, but low enough to crush the breath from his lungs.

Daphne clomped down on all fours gasping. "He knows better than that," his wife said. It was such a cold-blooded blow that I reacted.

"Maybe if you'd give him half a chance—" I said.

"I'd wind up as a niece," she snapped at me. *Wait until you see what happens to them.*"

"Shut up!" Daphne rolled to his side doubled up and glared at Annellica. "Shut up, Nellie, before I kill you."

I left the domestic tableau to resolve itself and sought my cabin. I stayed there through the remainder of the heavy acceleration, but when we went into free flight the Major dragged me out.

The party was still in full force with the three other girls doing titivating push-offs from wall to wall, convoluting their lovely bodies into incredible ballet formations, which Daphne took keen delight in disrupting with licentious hands—like a spoiled child pricking colorful balloons. Each fiasco ended in shrieks of laughter and mock combat, until the Major was snugged back in his hold-down strap, promising to behave.

Frequently he would raise his arms and aim an imaginary rifle. "Ka-chunk! Broke a leg that time. Ka-chunk! Right in the hip!" Then he'd holler over at me, "Never gut-shoot 'em. Break a bone."

Annellica remained bored and indifferent to the revelry. She drank sparingly and passed up a hundred opportunities to be alone with me. She paid meticulous attention to her husband's wants with the quiet efficiency and anticipation of a trained secretary, but I caught her eyeing me with a most provocative, speculating look. My experience with married virgins was too limited to interpret her glances.

All revolved around the Major. When he ate, we all ate. When he over-drank and slept, we slept.

I never did discover which three nieces were supposed to be "mine." None paid me any attention, and Daphne, much to my relief, never insisted upon my activity in his Bacchanalian affairs.

BEFORE we arrived at Tigursh II I was quite fed up with my host, drunk or sober. His indefatigable, sensual tastes wore on my nerves, but I still had no conception of the Roman carnival this was to turn into.

We touched down a few hundred yards from my prospecting camp, which was located at the edge of the two-hundred-mile plain. Daphne stowed the girls in their rooms like so many playthings, and the faceless captain announced that the ramp was down.

At the first smell of the hot, humid, over-rich air, the Major rared back his head and said, "I like it!"

I had forgotten the rather exhilarating effect of the high-oxygen content. Coupled with the low-gravity, Tigursh II induced a mild euphoria on its human visitors. My planet was small and dense, and the rapid rotation—once every seven and a half-hours—made for violent, capricious air currents and weather.

"I'll hike over to the compound and check on my crew," I told Daphne as the three of us bounced down the ramp.

"Don't bother," he said imperiously. "We passed them on the way in. Meant to tell you. I've been checking on them. You've got a nice thorium deposit, but it's a mile under that mud down there in the jungle." He waved carelessly to the south.

"You what?" I said incredulously.

"They were dissatisfied," Daphne said. "I gave them a furlough with pay. Like to have a place to myself, y'know."

"What goddam right did you have to—"

"Right?" He rolled the word around in his mouth as if it were a brand new concept. Then he chuckled. "Quit crying. They wanted off. I sent my ship after them. Saved you a hunk of cash. Hauled their samples back, too."

When I failed to respond he continued, "Let's not spoil the trip over it. Tell you what. I'll buy the mineral rights from you. How's that?"

"For a cold billion dollars," I said without thinking. He didn't bat a lash.

"Throw in the exclusive hunting rights and it's a deal," he said.

"She's yours to the core," I said quickly, "minerals, animals and vegetables." The cost of mining the thorium was completely beyond my means and my previous efforts to sell the whole planet had met with offers of less than a tenth of this amount.

He tilted his head back to glance at Annellica. "Get that? Easy to remember. A round billy for the parcel." She nodded, and he turned back to me. "Congratulations, Frost. Now you're a billionaire. Let's eat. I'm hungry."

Annellica produced a small hamper and followed along behind us as we strolled over toward the heavy greenery. I was still feeling weak. Having your only planet jerked from beneath your feet was not an experience I especially savored, in spite of the profit I realized. It gave me a better insight to Annellica's answer to my question. "Love? What has that to do with—anything?"

What Daphne wanted was his. He didn't need the minerals, and he was here at my invitation for the hunting. But—let's not have any unpleasantness. Spend a billion, and keep things friendly.

HE spotted a herd of heavy animals grazing a quarter of a mile away. Squatting, he waved us down in the deep grass. "We'll eat here," he said. "Keep an eye on those herbivores. They're close to the trees. See if anything comes after them."

Centaurus was a faint, golden ball above a high overcast. It was never meridian in the summer season, so the orb hung well up from the murky horizon to the south.

Daphne seemed unaffected by the oxygen, but I had a feeling of well being that approached intoxication. Annellica moved between us spreading the lunch. For the first time on the trip I felt genuinely hungry and began popping morsels into my mouth before she was finished laying it out.

I ate alone, however. The Major said, "I think I see a wampus."

Without a word, Annellica departed and returned in a minute with two rifles. Strapped to her side was one of the "nasty little nuclear pistols" that her husband deplored. He took one of the rifles and lined out the telescopic sight in the direction of the herd. I continued eating until he ejaculated, "Blitzmachen!"

On my knees, I could see a brief commotion in the herd, and the gusty wind brought the wavering sounds of grunts and a shrill neighing. A flash of bright orange tore back for the jungle dragging one of the smaller, lumpy herbivores that would have weighed half a ton on earth.

So I was right. There was interesting big game on Turgish II. Daphne sank into a tense silence. Annellica dropped beside me but didn't eat. She sat on her legs, hands folded in her lap while I rustled through the edible hungrily.

Finished, I stretched out in the dry grass that crackled under me, intending to take a nap. Daphne turned his head and whispered with irritation, "You people are making too much noise. Go on back to the ship until I get a line on what we're after."

His wife shrugged, and we turned back, leaving the picnic debris with Daphne.

When we reached the ship, she tossed her head and breathed deeply. "I like it out here. The air—it's—wonderful."

We sought the shade on the far side, out of view of the crouching Major and lay side by side facing each other. It was the first time we had been alone since the moment in the gallery. I was determined not to upset her again, but she kept her gaze on my eyes, waiting, expectant.

This time I answered *her* unasked question. "No. You're oxygen drunk. Besides, there's no future in it," I said bluntly.

"I know him," she said softly. "He won't return until dark. This may be our last chance to—to find out about each other."

"Find out what?"

Her lips drew into a faint pout. "Aren't you curious—about me?"

While I was strangling for an answer she went on, "And I must discover whether you are worth doing now what I must do some day." Her lips were tight now.

"What is that?"

She didn't answer, but she moved her head closely until her breath was sweet in my nostrils. My discretion vanished and I reached for her. Our lips met but she held our bodies apart with her hands.

It was quite different. The kiss was long and exploring and thoughtful and when my pressure against her fending hands grew more than she could bear she rolled free and jumped to her feet.

"It is worth it," she declared looking down at me with clenched fists and wide eyes, and for the first time I understood why the Major remained married to this lovely creature in spite of her rejection of him.

Watching her graceful limbs as she mounted the ramp I felt sorry for Daphne, an emotion I had thought impossible. But here was a man, foolishly wealthy in every respect but the one that counted most.

My pity was short-lived.

The night was short, but we slept less than half of it. Daphne chattered about the orange animal excitedly and made plans for the hunt.

"There are few of them around these parts," he said, "or else the herds of herbivores would be wiped out. We'll have to stake out bait to draw one, probably. Usually have to anyway."

HE cleaned his rifle four times and paced the salon impatiently awaiting dawn. Finally he glanced at his chronometer and told his wife, "Get Suchane—the darkest one. See that she's scrubbed down, well. No perfume, understand?"

It was the first time he had mentioned one of the girls to Annellica by name and she paled. I wondered why taking a "niece" on the hunt with us bothered her after the comportment I had witnessed on the trip.

In a half-hour the four of us set out in the first pale light of a dawn that exploded quickly into pink daylight. The Major wore a wicked hunting-knife in his belt, carried only a pint flask in his right hand and his left arm was wrapped intimately around Suchane's slender waist. Annellica carried the rifles.

We had gone only a few yards when he stopped us. "You wait here," he said. Then he sipped from the flask and offered it to the beautiful, dark-haired girl. She drank deeply and handed it back. He waved it to her with his satyr-like smirk, that she finish it. He watched until she was through, then his left hand slid up to her neckline, grasped the material of the dress and tore down with one powerful gesture.

She staggered back, nude and startled. Daphne roared with laughter, clasped her around the waist again and held out his right hand. "Nellie, my rifle. You wait here. Keep your heads down. No fair peeking, eh, Suchane?"

Annellica threw one of the two rifles she was carrying at him, muzzle up. He caught it with a slap of his huge paw and pulled the girl forward with him. She was reassured, now, and giggling with anticipation.

Somehow the lecherous display was more revolting out here in daylight. I mistook Annellica's paleness for humiliation, and I didn't blame her. Why did he have to drag one of his damned concubines out here?

We knelt down obediently, and before Daphne's head disappeared he turned and shouted back, "If the wampus gets by me, remember, no gut shots, Frost."

I muttered to Annellica, "The man has nerve, anyway."

"You confuse bravery with selfishness. He insists on the first shot—won't trust another member of a hunting party to hold his fire. He always stalks out ahead like this," Annellica explained tensely.

I had noticed that the niece carried no weapon. Which brought up another question. "Does he always mix his pleasures?" I asked.

She was in the act of withdrawing a long telescopic sight which she must have had bound to the inside of her thigh. As she mounted it to her rifle with feverish haste she answered, "He is not mixing his pleasures. *Suchane is bait.*"

Before this could sink in completely a shrill, feminine scream tore faintly into the gusty wind and found us. I leaped to my feet. Half way to the edge of the jungle, some hundred yards from us, I watched Daphne pushing the olive-skinned girl ahead of him with rough shoves. A deeper color spread from her neck and swathed one shoulder and her side.

He stopped and raised the rifle threateningly. She turned and fled toward the jungle.

"What in God's name—" I shouted.

"You can't help her," Annellica said hopelessly. "He's cut her jugular. If there's an animal in there the blood scent will bring it out in seconds. If there isn't—Suchane is gone, anyway."

I stared down at my companion in horror. She had warned me about the "Fate of Daffy's nieces," but I couldn't have visualized anything this bestial.

She looked up at me. "She will faint soon. There are worse ways to die. You will see." She arose to stand beside me.

I threw my rifle to my shoulder, fully intending to fire the whole clip into Daphne's back, but three things happened at once. Suchane sank out of sight in the grass, an orange splotch ripped into the open, and the Major, too, sank down and leveled his rifle.

The animal, even at this distance, was undoubtedly one of the Major's wampus varieties. It was stilt-legged, but not clumsy like a giraffe. The long, thick neck swung left and right tracing the scent of warm blood, and its cat-like body arched so high a man could have walked under it.

The wind was directly at our back, and as the several human scents touched the animal's nostrils it jerked the long-fanged mouth. Its belly touched the high grass in a quick crouch, then it sprang in one, deadly accurate leap that carried it forty yards to the prostrate Suchane. Even in the light gravity, the orange blur did not rise in a high trajectory, and the Major had time for only one shot while it was in the air.

The sound startled the beast as it settled on its prey, and it raised its ugly head high while Daphne slammed the rest of his ammunition at it with no effect.

Annellica stood calmly as her husband dropped his rifle unbelievingly. The heavy caliber bullets had failed to cause a quiver in the beast, but the shocking noise had made him nervous.

At the moment when it seemed he would turn and run for the jungle, Annellica raised her rifle. Daphne saw her sight through the telescope. "It's no use," he yelled. "We need higher power charges. Got a hide on him like a—"

She pulled the trigger.

The great animal pirouetted, bit at its own side, then wheeled facing us. Even as it sprang, Daphne, who was only twenty yards from us, screamed, "You gut-shot it! You clumsy—"

His wife dropped her rifle instantly after the shot and drew the little nuclear pistol. I got off one shot as the beast reached the apex of its leap, but I think I missed.

I kept waiting for Annellica's deadly hand-weapon to speak, but she followed the arc of the raking talons all the way to the ground where they churned briefly. Daphne only screamed once.

At last the pistol spat, just as the furry belly touched the grass in its third crouch. The leap came, but it was almost straight up. The slender pellet had entered the chest and cooked half the spine. The aimless floundering was reflexive spasm.

Annellica grabbed my rifle and fired three quick shots at the impervious hull of the ship. It brought the captain and two crewmembers to help us with the remains. Before they reached us, however, she was quick to secure Daphne's rifle and examine the chamber.

Even with an eyewitness and three other witnesses after the fact, she insisted that we hack the head and claws from the monster carnivore. We packed them, together with her husband's shredded corpse in the game freezer.

When a financial personage of Daphne's stature dies on a strange planet the investigation is most thorough. It wasn't necessary to take such pains with Suchane's pitiful remains. We buried her on Tigursh II where investigators could exhume her ripped body if they chose. The jugular slash was indistinguishable in the general lacerations.

It was a nasty mess. It cured me from any slight pleasure in hunting and cost me the quickest billion dollars I ever had a chance at.

Naturally, the deal was off without the Major to verify the verbal agreement. Anyway, with characteristic selfishness, he died intestate which threw all his holdings into the courts.

But the greatest change the incident made in my life concerned the loss of my, bachelorhood. A man can get his belly full of anything, even promiscuity, and Daphne's little hunting party did me that favor.

I'm still stuck with Tigursh II and its mile-under-mud thorium deposit and orange-colored wampuses but I have prospects. If the courts clear up the Daphne estate my wife will own more planets than I have golf balls.

So, if you ever go big game hunting again don't forget the Major's advice. I pass it on to you for what it's worth, although you may never aim at anything but a lion. Never gut-shoot a wampus. It's better even if you're only shooting blanks!

And I don't feel a damn bit bad about the way Annellica loaded the major's gun...

THE END

The Guest Rites

By ROBERT SILVERBERG

Carthule was not the Earthman's god, but Carthule protected him while he was a guest in the temple—even if he tore the temple down!

IT WAS TIME for the after-meal meditation. Marik, First Priest of Carthule, finished his frugal meal and went outside to sit in the mid-day breeze and watch the sands blowing gently over the bare flat plains. The problem of the Revelation occupied his reveries: why had Carthule, in His infinite wisdom, waited so long to reveal to His people that they were not alone in the universe?

Marik looked up at the glowing dot behind the gray wall of the sky. That, he knew, was the Sun. And there were other planets, some inhabited, some not. Carthule was not alone; He was one of nine. And His people had never suspected the truth until the flaming ships of the third planet—Earth, was it?—had broken through the skies, and the small white people had told them of the other worlds.

The problem was one which the greatest theologians of the time—in whose number Marik, without pride, deemed himself—had discussed at great length, never coming to a solution. Marik and Polla San, of the neighboring temple, had finally concluded that Carthule moved in ways too complex for His mortal people to understand.

Marik lowered his gaze from the sky and looked out across the dry expanse of desert. He could make out, dimly, Polla San's temple far across the sands. Polla San was due to visit him shortly, he recalled. Or was it the other way around? Marik frowned; he was getting old, and soon would have to relinquish his duties to one of the younger acolytes and spend his remaining decades sitting dreaming in the afternoon.

Calmly Marik settled into the semi-somnolence of the after-meal meditation, fixing his gaze on the far-off temple of Polla San but turning his vision inward. The sand blew in widening circles, until it seemed to Marik that there was a small, dark figure wandering out in the desert. Sleepily he watched the circlings of the small figure as it pursued a crazy path through the desert.

Then perception broke through his meditation and he realized something was in the desert that had no business there. Carefully he lifted the transparent nictitating lid that protected his eyes from the sand and focused sharply on the figure in the desert.

It was an Earthman! Lost in the desert, apparently. Marik, somewhat annoyed at this interruption of his meditation, rang for Kenra Sarg.

The young acolyte appeared immediately. Marik nodded. "Look out there," he said.

Kenra Sarg turned and stared. After a moment he turned back to Marik.

"That's an Earthman lost out there! We'd better bring him in here before he gets buried by the sand. What do you say, Father?"

"Of course, Kenra Sarg, of course. Bring him here."

The younger priest bowed and trotted out to the desert. Marik watched him as he ran. He was tall and powerful, and his skin was deep blue, almost purple. His powerful thigh muscles clenched and unclenched as he ran. *He reminds me of my younger self.* Marik thought, as he watched Kenra Sarg pound effortlessly over the sand. *He will be a fine successor when I am ready to go.*

He sank back into reverie, hoping for some repose before Kenra Sarg returned with the Earthman.

HE WAS SMALL, even smaller than the other Earthmen Marik had seen, and his mouth worked curiously and constantly. His face had been dried by the desert. He shook sand from his hair, his eyes, his ears.

"I thought I was finished that time," he said, looking up into Marik's eyes. The Earthman's eyes were bright and hard, and Marik found the contact unpleasant.

"You are safe here," Marik said. "This is the Temple of Carthule."

"I've heard of you people," the Earthman said. "Understand you're a sort of hotel and religion combined."

"Not exactly," Marik said. "But the strongest tenet of our faith is that the Guest Rite is inviolable. Our greatest joy is giving sanctuary to wanderers. You are welcome here so long as you care to stay."

The little Earthman nodded his head. "Sounds fine with me. But I won't trouble you long. I was just passing through this region on my way back to New Chicago—I mean Corolla—when I got lost in your desert. Dropped my compass in the sand and couldn't find my way after that."

"Yes," Marik said. "It is very difficult."

"You're telling me! It would not be so bad if you had stars here on Venus—Carthule, I mean—but you don't, and so there's no way to get your direction. I could have died out there before I found my way back to Corolla. I'm shipping back to Earth," he said. "I can't wait to get back. No disrespect meant, of course," he added cautiously.

Marik looked down at the Earthman. *I'll never get used to their pale skins, he thought. And they talk so much.* "Yes," he said. "I know many of your people find our planet a difficult one to live on. We are better adapted for such life than you."

"Sure," the Earthman said. "Say, could I get some rest now? I'm pretty well shot after that tour of your desert."

"Certainly," said Marik. "Kenra Sarg, will you show our guest to one of our rooms? Feel free to stay as long as you care to," he said to the Earthman. "Carthule's generosity is unbounded."

"Oh, don't worry about that," the Earthman said. "I'm not going to stay for long. Just a day or so to recover my bearings, so to speak, and once I'm in traveling shape again I'm heading straight for Corolla." Kenra Sarg led him away, and he followed, still talking.

Marik looked briefly up at the sky, but Carthule made no answer. For some reason Marik felt suspicious of this Earthman, and as he moved toward the room of prayer to perform the service customary upon the arrival of one seeking sanctuary, he uttered a small, silent plea to Carthule to keep his mind free of groundless hatreds.

WHEN MARIK finished his devotion before the great purple figure of Carthule, he kissed the blazing eye of the statue as was his private custom, humbled himself before the altar, and turned to leave.

"I waited till you were through, Marik," said a tall figure in priestly robes who had been standing at the door. "I didn't want to interrupt your service."

"Polla San! Why have you come here now? I expected you next month!"

Marik looked anxiously at his fellow priest. He knew well that the old priest of the neighboring temple left his books and his meditations infrequently, and never came to visit Marik without first sending notice.

"Serious business," said Polla San. Marik noticed for the first time that the other was wearing the gold band. It was a sign of deep sorrow.

"Tell me outside," Marik said. "This is not the room for it."

"This is of His realm," Polla San said. "Listen: not long ago one of the Earthmen arrived at my temple. He said he was on his way to Corolla, and was looking for shelter and a place to sleep before crossing the desert. Of course, we welcomed him and, since we had no more beds, I gave him my room and slept on the floor in the meal room. Last night he left, hurriedly, without telling anyone. When I found my room empty, I concluded he had gone, and I went to the room of prayer to offer my wish that Carthule protect him on his journey. I bowed before the statue, even as you did now—and when I looked up I saw that the eye had been stolen!"

"No!" Marik said. He turned and looked at his own statue of Carthule. In the center of the forehead burned the irreplaceable stone that had been set there century upon century before—a great red stone with secret fires burning in its heart. He tried to picture the eye not there, and could not. The eye was the heart of the Temple.

"Our Earthman had stolen the eye," Polla San said. "But he is still in our power. He left so hurriedly that he forgot this." He reached into his robe and took out a small metallic object.

"His compass," Polla San said. "Without this, he cannot cross the desert. He is still out there somewhere. Come: let your acolytes and mine search the desert for him, regain the eye, and give him the death he deserves."

Marik sank to his knees before the statue. "No," he said.

"No?" Polla San put his hand on the other's shoulder. "We are within our rights. The Earthmen will agree with us; he has committed a sacrilege and we must punish him for it. Why be afraid?"

"It's not that," Marik said. "He richly deserves death. But he is not in the desert. He is here."

"Here?"

"I saw him wandering out there and sent Kenra Sarg to bring him in. He is asleep in one of our guestrooms now. I was just performing the Guest Rite for him when you came."

Polla San sank to his knees alongside Marik. "This is serious, Marik. If he is a guest of yours, he is inviolate. He will sleep here in the home of Carthule after having committed the greatest of desecration's, and we must serve him and feed him and shelter him. It's not right, Marik!"

Marik turned in amazement. "You're not questioning the Word, are you? The Guest Rite is inviolable. As long as he is our guest, we cannot harm him. To punish him for his act would be a greater violation than the act itself."

"But can we let this Earthman remain a guest of Carthule, Marik? Let him sleep down there with the eye in his pocket, and not do a thing about it! He could flaunt the jewel under our noses and we'd have to nod our heads and offer him more food."

"The way of Carthule is the right way," Marik said. "The Guest Rite is inviolable. We will continue to treat this Earthman as we would Carthule Himself."

"But what can I do, Marik? My temple is no longer a temple without the eye!"

"Carthule will show us the way, Polla San. Suppose we pray."

THE FOLLOWING morning the Earthman, after a hearty meal, stretched himself luxuriously and looked out across the desert.

"I guess I'll be moving along," he said to Marik. "I'm in fine shape now, thanks."

"I am glad you found your stay restful," Marik said, concealing his feelings for the desecrator. "Carthule is ever-providing."

The Earthman began to move idly up and down the meal room, examining the ancient furnishings. "That reminds me," he said. "You wouldn't have a compass to lend me, would you?"

"A compass?" Marik let a puzzled frown cross his forehead. "What may a compass be?" he asked in just the right tone of ignorance.

The Earthman glanced at him impatiently. "You know," he said, gesturing with his hands. "It's a sort of a little metal box with a magnetic pointer. You must have seen them."

"No," Marik said. "Out here we rarely have guests from your world. I have not seen any compasses."

"Don't you use them yourselves—or something equivalent, I mean? A compass is for traveling. It tells you what direction you're going in."

Marik smiled. "We of Carthule have no need of such things, friend. We need no external guides here."

The Earthman worried a tangled wisp of hair. "Nothing at all? How do you find your way around in the desert?"

"We know how to travel," said Polla San quietly, emerging from his reverie.

"But—how can I get back to Corolla without a compass? I'll just get lost again!" The Earthman looked anxiously from one impassive blue face to another.

"Carthule will help you, friend," Marik said. "Carthule helps all who love Him!"

It seemed to Marik that the Earthman paled a little.

"Maybe you could lend me a guide," he said. "I can pay well. Maybe you could let me have that big fellow who brought me in from the desert? He could just show me the way to Corolla and then come right back."

"Our acolytes have no time for such journeys," Marik said. "We are busy here all the day long."

"But all you do is pray—I mean—" he broke off, realizing he had insulted his hosts. He turned and stared out at the shifting sands.

"You will have to set out alone," Polla San said.

"Can't you let me have anyone? Just a kitchen boy?" His hard little eyes flicked from one priest to the other. "Anyone at all? Otherwise I'm stuck here for good!"

"Carthule will guide you," Marik said.

The Earthman stared angrily at the tall priests. "I'm beginning to think you want me to get lost again," he said. "You talk about Carthule, and charity, but because I'm an Earthman you won't help me. But I'll show you. I'll get back to Corolla. And you'll pay for this when I do!"

He ran out. Marik and Polla, sitting quietly, exchanged glances.

"We are moving in the right direction," Polla San said. "But I think you would be wise to guard your room of prayer lest he seek to add to his collection."

"No fear of that," Marik said. "We'll see him again."

THE EARTHMAN disappeared later that morning. Kenra Sarg reported that he had set out, alone, in the general direction of Corolla, after fruitlessly attempting to bribe one of the kitchen boys to accompany him. He had offered them fabulous sums, but they had laughed at him.

The Eye of Marik's Carthule was still in place, but one of the younger acolytes, who had been praying all morning, told Marik that the Earthman had furtively entered the room of prayer and had backed out upon seeing the priest at his devotions.

With the Earthman gone, Marik returned to the calm of his daily routine. The after-meal meditation was a pleasant one; he and Polla San sat facing the desert, contemplating the grandeur of Carthule and pondering the meaning of His ways, until they sank into a transcendent peace. As the night winds began to cool the desert, they fell into a discussion of the problem of evil.

Marik maintained that Carthule had created the Earthmen out of His infinite wisdom, better to show the virtue of His people by contrast; while Polla San, wandering on the very edge of orthodox theology, suggested that the god whom the Earthman worshipped was actually independent of Carthule, representing the embodiment of evil as Carthule was the personification of good.

Marik refused to accept this, arguing that Carthule had created both His people and the Earthmen, or perhaps—as a concession to Polla San—that he had created the god of the Earthmen who, in turn, had created the Earthmen. The discussion went on through the night, while the night winds swirled the sand up around the temple, and they felt no need of sleep.

"Your theory denies the omnipotence of Carthule," Marik said, as the night winds began to lower in intensity. "If you postulate an evil force of as great power as the good, you deny the factors on which our morality—" Marik broke off, seeing that Polla San had slipped off into the near-sleep of a reverie.

He stood up, his long legs cramped after the afternoon and night of sitting, and walked up and down. The desert was settling into its morning calm after the tempestuous night. He stared, out across it, thinking of the Earthman who had set out for Corolla with the priceless eye of Carthule in a pouch by his side.

There was a figure in the distance, walking slowly and with great difficulty in widening circles, following a wild path to the temple. Marik lifted his nictitating lid to make sure his eyes were not playing him false.

Then, rather than awakening Kenra Sarg or Polla San, he did up his robe and went out in the desert to fetch the Earthman back himself.

HE HAD BEEN wandering all night, tossed by the night winds, eyes and ears and mouth choked with sand. He was still master enough of himself to throw an angry glare at Marik when the priest approached, but he suffered himself to be lifted like a child and carried back to the temple. The pouch was still hanging by his side, Marik noted.

"I see our friend has returned," Polla San said.

"Yes," Marik said. "Yesterday morning he departed without taking leave and lost his way again on the way to Corolla. After a night in the desert he found his way back to us and is once again looking for sanctuary. This is true, isn't it?" Marik said, looking down at the Earthman cradled in his arms.

The Earthman angrily spat out some sand.

"Carthule in His mercy has brought our wanderer back," Polla San said.

"I'll take him below," Marik said. "His night in the desert has left him weak and sore, and he needs rest. But he will always find sanctuary here with Carthule. Carthule shows His generosity to the lowest of creatures."

Kenra Sarg appeared at the door. "I see our guest has returned," he said.

"Yes. He has come back to us." Marik handed the Earthman over to Kenra Sarg, despite an impotent look of rage from the huddled, battered little thief.

"Take him to the room he had, and let him rest. He has traveled, and he is weary. I will go to the room of prayer, and offer up the Guest Rite for him, for he is our guest again. For as long as he cares to stay."

Kenra Sarg nodded and carried the Earthman inside.

Marik turned to Polla San. "Carthule has treated us well. I always feel happy when we have a guest."

Polla San smiled. "He still has the eye, I hope."

"He still does. I don't think he got too far last night. I've never seen anyone quite so angry."

"He will never find his way to Corolla alone," Polla San said. "Not without this." He thoughtfully fondled the compass in his hand.

"If my acolytes were not all so busy, I would allow one to guide him," Marik said, smiling. "But I can spare none, and I enjoy offering our hospitality. He is our guest, and we must do all in our power to make his stay enjoyable. Perhaps he will never want to leave."

"No," Polla San said, standing up and flexing his legs. "He will leave often, and silently. Perhaps he will take your statue's eye as well, to put in the pouch by his side. But he will return, as he did yesterday."

"He will return," Marik said. "Again and again. He will never find his way across the desert to Corolla, and eventually he will stay here as our permanent guest. And one day he shall die, if not sooner then later—these Earthmen are a short-lived breed and we will recover the eyes, which will still be in the pouch by his side."

"It is wonderful to have a guest," Polla San said.

"It is," Marik said. "He shall live here with the eyes by his side, and one day he will die and we can recover our treasures from him. He can never get far with them. We can wait. He has but a few decades left, while Carthule has all eternity. Come," he said. Together they went to the room of prayer to offer the service of the Guest Rites.

THE END

Journey for the Brave

By ALAN E. NOURSE

Courage will be a big qualification for the pilot who flies the first moon rocket. But who decides if a man is brave—or a coward...?

THE base diner was hot and stuffy that night as Scotty Johnson sat with Mitch and Jack and the other boys, sipping his last cup of coffee before Zero Hour rolled around. Mitch and Jack had succeeded in sneaking him out of town before the reporters had guessed what was happening. Now they sat in silence, sipping their coffee, glancing at him from time to time as though to make sure he were still there. It annoyed Scotty. This was the time to laugh, and joke, and bull away as if nothing was going to happen at all.

The waitress trotted over with a coffeepot, and Scotty gave her his widest leer. "You know, I can't think of anything I'd rather have right now than a cup of coffee from you," he said. "How about a date in about ten days?"

The girl looked startled and glanced away nervously. Mitch gave a tight little laugh. "Better watch out, Scotty. She's liable to be waiting on the landing field when you get back—"

They all laughed at that, and then silence fell again. They were nervous. Scotty could sense it, even though they tried to cover it up. All through these weeks of preparation in the hot New Mexico sun, the tension had been growing. But he should be the one to be nervous, not these lads. After all, who was the star of this show? Scotty nuzzled his coffee, and twisted his wiry five-foot-two inch frame around so that he could see the door. "Better drink up," he said. "The jeep should be here any minute."

Mitch nodded and emptied his cup as the jeep's tires screeched on the pavement outside. The coffee shop door opened and a head with an MP's crash helmet popped in. "All set, Scotty? Let's go!"

Scotty nodded. His blue eyes were bright as he buttoned up his jacket and winked at the waitress. Then he led the group to the door. "Love that gal," he said.

The driver raced the motor as they piled in and the jeep took off down the concrete strip with a roar. The driver turned an admiring glance toward Scotty. "All set for the big trip, man?"

Scotty grinned. "Been sleeping in a coffin all week, just for practice."

"Man, you may need that practice. You'll be good and stiff before you get out——" He broke off, horrified at the pun.

Scotty roared with glee. "You think you're kidding! That's all right—the way I see it, I'm getting ten days vacation on the Government, and plenty of pay besides. And once I get up there, I won't need much muscle to make my way around, they tell me." He lit a cigarette, peering down the strip ahead of them. Far ahead he could see the batteries of searchlights, picking out the tall, shiny spire of the ship. It stood tall in its scaffolding, pointing like a needle toward the black star-lit sky. Already the ground below it was swarming with tiny figures, moving about on the final check-down. My ship, thought Scotty. I helped to build it. And here's one job where they need a cocky, loudmouthed little shrimp more than anything else in the world——

ANOTHER jeep swerved in beside them on the strip. Scotty caught a glimpse of the General and a couple of official-looking civilians.

"Everybody's going to see you off," said Mitch from the back seat.

"Yeah—the whole damned crowd. My big day."

"You sure you got everything down cold?"

Scotty gave him a scornful glance. "You kidding? How could I miss?" His freckled face broke into a grin from ear to ear, and his eyes were bright with excitement. "Why I've got

138

nothing to do but crawl in and zip things up after me. Don't even have to throw the fatal switch—they take care of everything from outside. I'm telling you, it's a cinch. Three days to tell myself sea stories—and then I'll crawl out and tell you boys what Lady Moon *really* looks like."

A crowd of reporters and photographers were waiting as the jeep sped up to the huge barbed-wire enclosure surrounding the ship. Scotty stuck his head out of the jeep and gave them a big grin. The flashbulbs popped. Then the jeep roared on toward the field shack. Scotty stepped out, staring up at the tall sleek ship. A little bottom-heavy now, perhaps, but with the first and second stages disengaged—a beauty of a ship. He stepped into the field shack, and grinned up at the General. "Final check go all right?"

The General nodded and smiled. "This is the Secretary of Defense, Scotty—"

"Well! Guess I'm rating big visitors tonight!" He gave the man's hand a jaunty shake.

"You're taking a big trip," said the Secretary. "Tell me, Mr. Johnson—how does it feel to be the first man to go to the Moon?"

"Can't say. I haven't been there yet."

"You'd better get aboard," said the General. "Everything's been checked down. You'll have half an hour to make your own checks from inside. How's your weight?"

"Down to 128."

"Fine. That's better than we'd hoped. But don't be afraid to holler if something doesn't look right—" He extended his hand, gripped Scotty's tightly. "Good luck, lad. We're with you all the way."

A soldier rode up the gantry with him, high up past the break-lines of the first and second stages, to the small open port in the final stage of the rocket. Scotty could feel the eyes on him from below as he climbed into the port—one lone man to jockey the first manned ship to the Moon. A big job; a job that really took guts. He grinned, and slid through into the passenger chamber. Carefully he reached back and slammed the port shut behind him with a farewell wave to the soldier, and gave the lock-wheel a spin, until he heard the seal click. Then he slipped down into the half-sitting, half-reclining couch, which nearly filled the tiny chamber. His heart was pounding in his throat as he snapped on the radiophone. "Okay, I'm in," he said.

"Got her locked up?" Mitch's voice grated in his earphones.

"Ay, ay."

"Give her a careful check inside there. Then stand by."

Scotty nodded and checked the banks of instruments on the tiny panel before him. He was the payload on this trip; the ship was little more than an upholstered tube, with him jammed tight in one end and enough fuel to land him on the Moon and shoot him off again in behind him. The other sections, far huger than this little pellet with him in the middle, would drive him out, break the frightful hold that Earth held on her subjects. But there was nothing superfluous here, nothing he did not actually need, and he checked quickly. Then he leaned back and flipped on the forward televiewer...

The vast black expanse of space, peppered with a thousand bright pinpoints of light, suddenly appeared on the screen inches from his face. It took him by surprise; his hand jerked down on the switch again, and he wiped a line of droplets from his upper lip, and closed his eyes, his heart pounding against his ribs.

The radio blipped in his ear. "Thirty minutes to Zero," it said—

IT struck Scotty Johnson, then, how very much alone he was.

He felt a chill go down his spine, and he turned his eyes about the tiny chamber. Forward, within arm's length, was the dull glint of metal paneling and coiled wires and tight atmosphere sealing. His small wiry body sank against the deep couch, and he drew the safety webbing across his chest and thighs, the chill in his mind deepening. Above him was another pad of soft material to protect his head; his feet were lodged against a solid bar at the foot of the couch. Inevitably, he thought of a cocoon. A tight, soft, warm cocoon. And he was alone inside it—

He tried to think when, in all his thirty-four years, he had been so completely and utterly alone.

He sat very still, listening. All about him was silence. A muted, deathly silence. His headset pressed tight against his ears, and he shook his head, wondering if he had actually heard the words coming into his ears a few seconds before. Zero minus thirty minutes. Thirty minutes to wait, alone—

Suddenly, he knew that he was very much afraid—

His lips formed a sneer, and he tried to fight the idea out of his mind. He was no longer afraid of anything. Those days were gone, far away. Nothing could scare Scotty Johnson—not even being completely alone. He reached out his hand, ran a finger over the control board. Oxygen, chamber pressure, emergency anaesthetic, blast-control—his hand trembled, and the thought seeped back into his mind again. A voice was whispering, deep in his ear, *you're afraid, little man, afraid*—! He could feel the droplets of moisture forming on his forehead, and even the sound of his breath was muted in the silent chamber.

The seconds ticked by. Still the voice whispered. He was alone—alone and afraid. No one could help him now, no one in the world. This was his own world, here in this tight little cabin, and he could die here and nobody would ever know—

He shook his head savagely. Alone? Ridiculous! At the foot of the ship were a hundred people, all watching, all thinking about him. They had built this ship, they were for him all the way. They would get him safely off the ground, and then it would be just like a subway ride—

But after the blast-off—what then? The hundred men were staying behind. There were no men where he was going. There was nothing there. Nothing but death.

His breath was coming faster, and he felt the first chill of panic stir in his mind. He tried to fight it down angrily. What was there to get excited about? Nobody had forced him into this seat. He'd begged for it! For five long years it had been an obsession, his wildest dream to be sitting in this seat, waiting for the Zero-count to come through the headphones. Years of hoping, of pulling strings, of talking to people and dropping chance remarks, of studying and working and practicing—and finally, the note in his box, the trip down to the General's field office that day.

INSIDE the office the General had sat down, regarding him for a long moment with those cool grey eyes of his. Then he said, "You're sure you want to do this, Scotty? Dead sure?"

Scotty had nodded, hardly able to find his voice. "I'd give anything. You've got to let me go."

The General nodded slowly. "You might have to give your life. Does it mean that much to you? Millions of dollars have gone into this ship, but there's no way to be sure of it. It's a fearful gamble."

"I'll take any odds, General. The sheep and the chickens came back. I'll come back."

The General looked out the window, his face carved with weary lines. "I hate to send a man, alone. But what we need to know, one man can find out. Two would be a waste—a tragic waste. The sheep and chickens didn't land, they just circled. But one man must go up, to land a ship, and take off again, for the first time." His eyes caught Scotty's gravely. "I want you to know why it's got to be you alone. We can't gamble on two men's lives, when one will do. *You're the guinea pig!*"

Scotty had stood up then, laughing. "Are you trying to frighten me? Look, General—I've been working on this ship since it first started. I know it inside out and backwards. I'm not afraid of this trip. I've got to be the one to go."

The General had shifted some papers on his desk. "All right. They weighed you in at 142 pounds. Our calculations call for

135. Every ounce over that cuts a hard percentage out of your fuel. You'll have to suck down."

"I can do that."

"All right—but don't starve yourself. And don't dehydrate any more than you absolutely must. You'll have enough water for ten days, no more. Three up, three back, four there. Now then. The psych boys will go to work on your coordination for the next few days. That's critical. The first and second stages will disengage automatically, but you'll have to maneuver your own landing."

Scotty nodded. "I've been maneuvering dummies until I'm blue in the face."

"You'll need it pounded in."

"It's pounded, don't worry."

The General gave a satisfied nod. "All right, Scotty. See you at the blast-off. And remember, if you want to pull out— nobody will blame you. Right down to the last minute before Zero, you can pull out—"

"I don't think so," said Scotty. "I don't think I'm going to pull out. Not on this one."

"ZERO minus twenty minutes— "

The harsh metallic voice dragged Scotty back to the present with a jolt. For a moment he had almost regained the old familiar burn of self-assured bravado he had felt as he had finished talking to the General that day and sauntered out toward the ship standing in the launching scaffold. He had even been smiling as he recalled the interview—

But now his eye caught the dull gleam of the control board before him, and his smile faded.

The voice was whispering softly, deep inside his head: *Come off it, Scotty. Who are you trying to kid?*

His hand trembled, and he leaned back, forcing his tense leg muscles to relax. What do you mean, who am I trying to kid? he thought, angrily. You're crazy. Would I be kidding myself? I quit kidding myself years ago. I know what I'm up to. This is a journey for heroes, and I'm going to be the hero, this time. *For sure.* This time there won't be any doubt. *They* won't have any doubt, and I won't have any doubt—

You're alone, Scotty. Remember? You can quit acting now.

He shuddered, and glanced uneasily around the tiny closed chamber. Alone? What a laugh. A man can never be alone. There are always a million memories, wheeling and spinning and roaring around inside your head. Memories of people, of hopes and dreams and fears. You can build a heavy wall in your mind to keep them back, but when you're alone, and scared, and helpless, the wall starts to crumble down—

There's nobody to fool any more, Scotty. The act is over. Admit it, you're scared, *you can hardly hold still you're so scared*—

He clapped his hands to his ears, trying to shut out the whisper. He kept shaking his head, but it came through like a heavy surf. He sat tense, trembling, with salty droplets pouring down his face, shaking his head helplessly—

You're caught now, the voice whispered. This is a one-way ride, and you know it, and you're *scared*—

"I'm not!"

The earphones clicked. "You say something, Scotty?"

Scotty took a deep breath, unclenching his hands. "No, no—nothing. What's the Zero-count, Mitch?"

"Zero minus sixteen minutes. Everything set?"

"All set. I wish we could get going." Scotty twisted on the couch, feeling the silence close down around him like a stifling blanket. He was almost shouting to himself. All right, I'm scared! Wouldn't anybody be scared? Sitting here, waiting, thinking about two hundred thousand miles of nothing with a rocky world of death at the other end to land on? Why shouldn't I be scared? They can stay back here, and track me with their scopes and radar—it's fine for them. It's fine for the Secretary of Defense, too—no skin off his back if something happens. And the big boys in Hollywood can sit back at their desks and rub their fat hands together and hope their cameras work all right, hope the pictures come out good, so they can make their pile, *if I get back*. Big gamble for them. FIRST MOON PICTURES RELEASED—SEE MAN'S GREATEST ADVENTURE IN GLORIOUS TECHNICOLOR— AUTHENTIC FILMS FROM THE FIRST MOON ROCKET—PRICES ONLY SLIGHTLY ADVANCED. Big gamble. Those films will help pay for a lot of fuel, a lot of metal and man-hours spent on this ship—

But can it pay for a life?

BITTERNESS swept through Scotty's mind, sharply. It was his life they were bartering, *he* was to be the star of those films—dead or alive. He could be killed in the blast-off, and the films would keep rolling, keep churning out the yardage, and thirty years later they could pick up the film and still make their nice safe pile—thirty years of cold death for him—

But why are you whining now, little man? Why all the tears, all of a sudden? You asked for it. You made your bed, right from scratch. You wanted to be the hero, nothing else would do. Well, here you are, Hero. Tough. You asked for it—

But *why?*

And then something was tugging at his mind, seeping through the heavy wall of memory. A terrible, loathsome thought. He shook his head, desperately, trying to fight it back, but the wall began to crumble. Long-dead pictures began drifting through, long-hidden memories. A bare whisper of thought, cold, relentless, devastating. Admit it, Scotty. *You had to come.* You had to be sitting in this seat; you couldn't do anything else, could you? You couldn't let them know about you. You couldn't bear to let the boys down on the field suspect the truth, could you, Scotty? You looked into their eyes, and you were afraid they suspected, like Matty had suspected, like Dad had suspected so many years ago— You had to come here. *You couldn't help yourself, could you?*

The whisper broke into a coarse, derisive laugh, and Scotty cowered back, shaking his head in denial, his whole body trembling. *Take a look, Scotty—take a good look!* Are you trying to hide the truth from *yourself?* But you can't get away with that. You can't hide it from yourself any longer—

And then the wall of memory buckled, and split wide open. You can fool the whole world, Scotty—but you can't fool yourself, the voice screamed in his ear. You can run, and hide, and twist, and lie, but you can't ever really fool yourself. You know it's true. You always have known.

You're a coward, Scotty. A dirty yellow coward. You always have been, and you always will be—

"Zero minus ten minutes—"

IT wasn't true. He shook his head helplessly as his fingers found the safety belts, tightened them down fiercely on his chest and legs. Wasn't he sitting here now, waiting for the last count, waiting to start on the greatest adventure man had ever attempted? Would he be *here* if he were a coward? He snarled and clenched his fists tight on the armrests. It was a lie, it *couldn't* be true. No man can stare himself in the face and call himself a coward when there is a spark of life left in him at all. He can call himself a cheat, or a liar, or a fake—those were things that could be changed, things that could be made up for. But a coward had something wrong deep inside, something that was built in, that could never be changed as long as a man lived. No man could call himself *that*.

Scotty shook his head, half laughing, half-crying. He was scared, sure. Anybody would be scared. But he wasn't a coward. He was in this ship because he wanted fame, because he craved excitement and adventure. Nothing had made him volunteer. He'd done it because he was that kind of guy—

But he knew that was a lie. Its very falsehood writhed in his brain as he thought it. You're here because your cheap, cowardly little soul couldn't bear to face itself. You're here because you couldn't bear the looks of the men around you with their barbed wise-cracks and their guarded half-smiles. They thought you couldn't see them! But the whispers were there, and you couldn't stand for them to guess—

But what did he care what *they* thought? What were they to him? *He* knew he was better than they were—quicker, smarter, braver. He didn't have to prove anything to them—

And Matty? Does Matty know how brave you are, Hero? Can you prove to Matty that you're not a coward? Matty knows about you. Remember?

Scotty shook his head, fearfully. That was so long ago—

But things like that are never long ago, Scotty. They stay with you as long as you live. Sure, the Army said you were a hero, they gave you a Silver Star—but what would Matty say—if he could ever say anything again? Would *he* say you were a hero?

Suddenly Matty's torn and twisted face seemed to be peering out at him from the control panel. His mind went whirling back through the years, completely out of control. In an instant he had slipped back fifteen long years, back to the hot, stinking sweaty deadliness of that little jungle island. They had been deep in the jungle that night, holed in, scared to move, afraid even to breath. For a week they had been waiting, waiting for the snipers to move in and spot them. He could remember the cold, desperate fear that had gnawed at him that night as he and Bill Matthews had clutched their rifles, waiting, creeping forward along the jungle trail through the blackness and the night sounds. His clothes had stuck to his body with sweat as they crept, the sweat of mortal fear. The mosquitoes whined in clouds around his head; his body stung with a thousand insect bites. Up ahead, somewhere in the sticky blackness, was a machine-gun, blocking them from their supplies, blocking them from the plasma and penicillin powder the patrol needed more than any food or water. They had been waiting for many days, and they were weak with hunger and thirst—but there was a gun, and sharp, cruel eyes watching—

THEY had been moving in pairs, and Scotty had felt the fear clutching his chest, fear beyond any words. He and Matty were working their way down a swampy river bottom, sliding on their bellies in the muck, when they had spotted the nest. And then the fear and panic building up inside him had broken through. He had jumped up, screaming, and burst forward, gun chattering in his hand.

Blind rage and fear drove him forward as the startled gunners swiveled their gun, piercing the night with their sharp cries. Matty had shouted at him to get down, but he ran forward in the darkness, wildly. A burst of fire screamed out at him through the jungle; he slid into the mud, panting, still firing into the face of the blazing machine gun, until he saw the last man twist, and fall, and the gun fell silent.

A hero, they said. But later he had found Matty, lying twisted with his head split open, a line of open holes cutting down through his neck and across his shoulders—

Another few seconds, another instant of control would have given them time to get the machine gun in crossfire. But something had exploded in Scotty's brain that night—a fear greater than any fear of being shot, a fear of being exposed for what he was, what he knew he was. He had dragged Matty back, through the long miles of sniper-ridden jungle, and they called him a hero, and he had never told them who had broken first and drawn the deadly fire—

His forehead stood out with sweat now, and he tried to hide his eyes. He had spent many years forgetting that horrible night, trying to cleanse himself of the depths of guilt that had eaten away at him—and now it was back, harsh and undeniable, intensified by years of self-deceit and self-justification and rationalization. But the chips were down now. In a few moments a great fire would explode deep in the bowels of this ship, and he would be driven forward, far out into space, along trails never blazed by man.

"Zero minus five minutes. Give her a final check, Scotty—"

He jerked in his seat as though he had been struck. *Five minutes!* His mind whirled with memories, and the cold fear cut through him like a knife. In a moment of panic his mind was screaming, get out, now, before it's too late! The General said you could pull out, right down to the last minute—well, *pull out, now, before the engines start*—

But a peal of derisive laughter roared through his mind. There had been reporters, news stories. He had said things that had been splashed across a million newspapers. Back out now? Tell the world what a coward he was? Then everybody would know—the boys down below, Matty, Dad—Dad had never actually *said* it, but it had always been there, as long as Scotty could remember. He had tried and tried to make up for his small size, for his skinny legs and bony chest.

It hadn't been his fault that Dad was such a big man, such a rugged, powerful man. Those long hunting trips up through Canada—a man had to share the load, there was no place for weakness and weariness there. And Dad had taken him along, once, until he had tired, and turned his ankle on a short portage. They had carried him out—and he knew that he had lost his Dad that day. Dad hadn't admitted it, but it was true. There was always the half-hidden disgust and sadness and disappointment in his cool, grey eyes—

"Minus two, Scotty. Final check—"

His hand flicked out automatically, as fear and dismay welled up in his mind. Everything he had ever done he had flubbed, somehow—he searched frantically through his mind for one small, pure act of absolute bravery, unadorned by words, unaltered by empty rationalizations and built-up courage, and his mind yielded nothing but hoarse, heavy laughter. Somewhere there was a key. It had started somewhere, if only he could remember. Somewhere beneath the years of futile failure there was a core—

"Sixty seconds, Scotty—Good luck, boy!"

He froze, his hands clutching the safety belt in a grip of iron as the words pounded in his ear: "—forty—thirty-five—thirty—twenty-five—"

And then, like a great door opening up in his mind, he remembered—

A DAY so long ago, so deeply buried that it had not come to mind in years. A day when he had been walking down a village street, on the way to the store for his mother, a small boy, hardly ten—

A group of boys, appearing suddenly from the old garage he was passing. A thin-faced lad, tall and sharp-boned, with cold eyes and a sneer on his thin lips. Other boys, too, mostly bigger than he. His eyes widened, and he started to back away when Thin-face grabbed his collar, pulled him up sharp. "Where you think you goin', bud?"

"Just down the street—"

"Who said you could walk on this street?"

"It's not your street. I can walk where I want—"

A gleam of cruelty in Thin-face's eyes. "Sissy thinks he's smart." A sharp-knuckled hand struck him across the nose. "You want to fight?"

Scotty shook his head, eyes wide. "No, I just want to—" His eye caught one of the others, sidling around behind him—

"Stand still!"

He had been paralyzed. The rabbit punch struck him a hammer-blow, and tears streamed down his face. Thin-face hit him again, and blood spurted from his nose. "Put up your hands and fight—"

"I can't—"

"You'd better fight, sissy—I'll kill ya!"

"I don't want to fight—" The fear, the mortification, the blind, paralyzing fear. Another blow struck him, and he tumbled backwards over the boy who had crouched behind him, and struck his head on the sidewalk. They had roared with laughter, and one of them kicked him. And then he was on his feet, darting between them, running for his life, running with blind fear snarling at his heels, down an alley, into a backyard, across into another alley— He had seen the open cellarway, then, and crawled down in, heart pounding in his throat, waiting as the boys came through the yard, looking, laughing at the sport, walking on. He waited for hours before he dared come out, and every minute of those hours he trembled, desperately sick and ashamed, wondering what Dad would ever think of him if he should find out—

SOMETHING struck him in the chest then, a firm, gentle pressure that grew and grew as the cabin vibrated with a powerful roar. The pressure grew larger, choking the breath from him. In a last terrible panic of fear Scotty tried to fight his safety belt open, tried to cry out to *stop, stop, stop*, but it was too late. He pressed back, deeper and deeper into the couch as the age-long seconds ticked by—and in the viewer the Earth fell away, farther and farther, dwindling, dimming—

He heard the explosion as the first stage disengaged, and his mind froze as the pressure shoved harder at his chest. Then suddenly there was a jerk, a bone-crushing jar that nearly broke his neck, and the ship started spinning crazily.

"Scotty—Scotty, can you hear me?" It was Mitch's voice in the earphones, heavy with frantic urgency. *"Can you hear me, Scotty?"*

Scotty groaned. "I can hear you," he croaked.

"Scotty, the second stage didn't disengage properly—you've got it on your tail yet—"

Scotty gasped for breath, trying to focus his mind on the present, trying to drive out the paralyzing phantoms of the past. "Second—stage?"

"It—wait a minute—you're way off course—there it goes, you've lost it—" There was a scraping sound in the earphones, and then the General's voice snapped out, sharp and clear. "Scotty—listen, boy, you're off-course, you aren't out far enough—you'll have to orbit back—"

"Orbit?" The word was wrenched from his throat, and he stared at the viewer in horror.

"Listen, Scotty, get this straight—can you hear me, lad?"

"Yeah, yeah, I can hear—"

"Then listen. Put your ship into orbit. Slam down the cut-off and—"

"I can correct," Scotty cried. "I can get back on beam, and make it—"

"Scotty, you'd use too much fuel. You didn't get out far enough, you dragged dead weight—"

"I can correct—"

"You'll never be able to land up there. If you do, you'll never be able to take off again—"

"I've—got—to—get—out—there!"

The General's voice was frantic. "This is an order, man. *Orbit your ship.* We'll find some way to get you down. But you'll have to come back—"

Something exploded in Scotty's mind then. Rage bubbled over in his mind, and he was screaming in the speaker, "I'm going on out. I'm going to land up there—I can't flub it now, I can't—"

"Scotty, *orbit while you can.* There'll be another try—"

"I can't hear you—"

"*I said—*"

"*I'm going out.* Get somebody up there to get me if you want to, but I'm going—"

He ripped off the earphones, the bitterness and rage and frustration of long years welling into his mind. He was seething, almost crying out in his rage. Everything he had ever done he had flubbed—but he wouldn't flub this one. Fiercely, he went to work on the controls, tears rolling down his cheeks as he worked. He was going to go on, if it killed him—

HE felt the ship respond to its new course, slightly, and then, gradually, the weight began to lift from his chest. He sank back, panting. Up in the screen was a pale yellow ball, and he was racing toward it as fast as a man could race. There would be plenty of time for the sensitive calculations, for careful course plotting, later. But he was not going back.

They might get a ship up to get him in time—and again, they might not. He had food and water for ten days at full rations.

He could live for thirty days on it. Maybe more. And when the rations were gone, how long could he live then?

How long did we live in the jungle without food or water?

He sat back, then, and laughed. It would be better to die up there, than to spend the rest of his life dying down on Earth. Dying every day, a thousand thousand deaths—

They might be able to rescue him, with fast work, with a fearful margin of incredible luck. But it didn't really matter to him now whether they did or didn't. He knew that now. He had already died, back there on the ground, waiting for the zero count to come. He was reborn now, a new man with a great, courageous job to do. This time he would do the job right. Fear was behind him now, for he could never be afraid again like he had been afraid a few short minutes before. The gauntlet was run.

He would land on the Moon, and neither man nor memory would stop him from doing it. No fear, no cowardice—

Because a coward would have turned back—

He settled back in the couch, and drifted into sleep with a peaceful smile on his lips.

THE END

Mr. Spaceship

By
PHILIP K. DICK

A human brain-controlled spacecraft would mean mechanical perfection.
This was accomplished, and something unforeseen: a strange entity called—

A brain in liquid with a trail coming out of it leading to a
spaceship. Left side image Right side image

Kramer leaned back. "You can see the situation. How can we
deal with a factor like this? The perfect variable."

"Perfect? Prediction should still be possible. A living thing still
acts from necessity, the same as inanimate material. But the cause-
effect chain is more subtle; there are more factors to be considered.
The difference is quantitative, I think. The reaction of the living
organism parallels natural causation, but with greater complexity."

Gross and Kramer looked up at the board plates, suspended on
the wall, still dripping, the images hardening into place. Kramer
traced a line with his pencil.

"See that? It's a pseudopodium. They're alive, and so far, a
weapon we can't beat. No mechanical system can compete with
that, simple or intricate. We'll have to scrap the Johnson Control
and find something else."

"Meanwhile the war continues as it is. Stalemate. Checkmate.
They can't get to us, and we can't get through their living
minefield."

Kramer nodded. "It's a perfect defense, for them. But there still
might be one answer."

"What's that?"

"Wait a minute." Kramer turned to his rocket expert, sitting
with the charts and files. "The heavy cruiser that returned this
week. It didn't actually touch, did it? It came close but there was no
contact."

"Correct." The expert nodded. "The mine was twenty miles off.
The cruiser was in space-drive, moving directly toward Proxima,

154

line-straight, using the Johnson Control, of course. It had deflected a quarter of an hour earlier for reasons unknown. Later it resumed its course. That was when they got it."

"It shifted," Kramer said. "But not enough. The mine was coming along after it, trailing it. It's the same old story, but I wonder about the contact."

"Here's our theory," the expert said. "We keep looking for contact, a trigger in the pseudopodium. But more likely we're witnessing a psychological phenomena, a decision without any physical correlative. We're watching for something that isn't there. The mine decides to blow up. It sees our ship, approaches, and then decides."

"Thanks." Kramer turned to Gross. "Well, that confirms what I'm saying. How can a ship guided by automatic relays escape a mine that decides to explode? The whole theory of mine penetration is that you must avoid tripping the trigger. But here the trigger is a state of mind in a complicated, developed life-form."

"The belt is fifty thousand miles deep," Gross added. "It solves another problem for them, repair and maintenance. The damn things reproduce, fill up the spaces by spawning into them. I wonder what they feed on?"

"Probably the remains of our first-line. The big cruisers must be a delicacy. It's a game of wits, between a living creature and a ship piloted by automatic relays. The ship always loses." Kramer opened a folder. "I'll tell you what I suggest."

"Go on," Gross said. "I've already heard ten solutions today. What's yours?"

"Mine is very simple. These creatures are superior to any mechanical system, but only because they're alive. Almost any other life-form could compete with them, any higher life-form. If the yuks can put out living mines to protect their planets, we ought to be able to harness some of our own life-forms in a similar way. Let's make use of the same weapon ourselves."

"Which life-form do you propose to use?"

"I think the human brain is the most agile of known living forms. Do you know of any better?"

"But no human being can withstand outspace travel. A human pilot would be dead of heart failure long before the ship got anywhere near Proxima."

"But we don't need the whole body," Kramer said. "We need only the brain."

"What?"

"The problem is to find a person of high intelligence who would contribute, in the same manner that eyes and arms are volunteered."

"But a brain...."

"Technically, it could be done. Brains have been transferred several times, when body destruction made it necessary. Of course, to a spaceship, to a heavy outspace cruiser, instead of an artificial body, that's new."

The room was silent.

"It's quite an idea," Gross said slowly. His heavy square face twisted. "But even supposing it might work, the big question is whose brain?"

It was all very confusing, the reasons for the war, the nature of the enemy. The Yucconae had been contacted on one of the outlying planets of Proxima Centauri. At the approach of the Terran ship, a host of dark slim pencils had lifted abruptly and shot off into the distance. The first real encounter came between three of the yuk pencils and a single exploration ship from Terra. No Terrans survived. After that it was all out war, with no holds barred.

Both sides feverishly constructed defense rings around their systems. Of the two, the Yucconae belt was the better. The ring around Proxima was a living ring, superior to anything Terra could throw against it. The standard equipment by which Terran ships were guided in outspace, the Johnson Control, was not adequate. Something more was needed. Automatic relays were not good enough.

—Not good at all, Kramer thought to himself, as he stood looking down the hillside at the work going on below him. A warm wind blew along the hill, rustling the weeds and grass. At the bottom, in the valley, the mechanics had almost finished; the last elements of the reflex system had been removed from the ship and crated up.

All that was needed now was the new core, the new central key that would take the place of the mechanical system. A human brain, the brain of an intelligent, wary human being. But would the human being part with it? That was the problem.

Kramer turned. Two people were approaching him along the road, a man and a woman. The man was Gross, expressionless, heavy-set, walking with dignity. The woman was—He stared in surprise and growing annoyance. It was Dolores, his wife. Since they'd separated he had seen little of her....

"Kramer," Gross said. "Look who I ran into. Come back down with us. We're going into town."

"Hello, Phil," Dolores said. "Well, aren't you glad to see me?"

He nodded. "How have you been? You're looking fine." She was still pretty and slender in her uniform, the blue-grey of Internal Security, Gross' organization.

"Thanks." She smiled. "You seem to be doing all right, too. Commander Gross tells me that you're responsible for this project, Operation Head, as they call it. Whose head have you decided on?"

"That's the problem." Kramer lit a cigarette. "This ship is to be equipped with a human brain instead of the Johnson system. We've constructed special draining baths for the brain, electronic relays to catch the impulses and magnify them, a continual feeding duct that supplies the living cells with everything they need. But—"

"But we still haven't got the brain itself," Gross finished. They began to walk back toward the car. "If we can get that we'll be ready for the tests."

"Will the brain remain alive?" Dolores asked. "Is it actually going to live as part of the ship?"

"It will be alive, but not conscious. Very little life is actually conscious. Animals, trees, insects are quick in their responses, but they aren't conscious. In this process of ours the individual personality, the ego, will cease. We only need the response ability, nothing more."

Dolores shuddered. "How terrible!"

"In time of war everything must be tried," Kramer said absently. "If one life sacrificed will end the war it's worth it. This ship might get through. A couple more like it and there wouldn't be any more war."

They got into the car. As they drove down the road, Gross said, "Have you thought of anyone yet?"

Kramer shook his head. "That's out of my line."

"What do you mean?"

"I'm an engineer. It's not in my department."

"But all this was your idea."

"My work ends there."

Gross was staring at him oddly. Kramer shifted uneasily.

"Then who is supposed to do it?" Gross said. "I can have my organization prepare examinations of various kinds, to determine fitness, that kind of thing—"

"Listen, Phil," Dolores said suddenly.

"What?"

She turned toward him. "I have an idea. Do you remember that professor we had in college. Michael Thomas?"

Kramer nodded.

"I wonder if he's still alive." Dolores frowned. "If he is he must be awfully old."

"Why, Dolores?" Gross asked.

"Perhaps an old person who didn't have much time left, but whose mind was still clear and sharp—"

"Professor Thomas." Kramer rubbed his jaw. "He certainly was a wise old duck. But could he still be alive? He must have been seventy, then."

"We could find that out," Gross said. "I could make a routine check."

"What do you think?" Dolores said. "If any human mind could outwit those creatures—"

"I don't like the idea," Kramer said. In his mind an image had appeared, the image of an old man sitting behind a desk, his bright gentle eyes moving about the classroom. The old man leaning forward, a thin hand raised—

"Keep him out of this," Kramer said.

"What's wrong?" Gross looked at him curiously.

"It's because I suggested it," Dolores said.

"No." Kramer shook his head. "It's not that. I didn't expect anything like this, somebody I knew, a man I studied under. I remember him very clearly. He was a very distinct personality."

"Good," Gross said. "He sounds fine."

"We can't do it. We're asking his death!"

"This is war," Gross said, "and war doesn't wait on the needs of the individual. You said that yourself. Surely he'll volunteer; we can keep it on that basis."

"He may already be dead," Dolores murmured.

"We'll find that out," Gross said speeding up the car. They drove the rest of the way in silence.

For a long time the two of them stood studying the small wood house, overgrown with ivy, set back on the lot behind an enormous oak. The little town was silent and sleepy; once in awhile a car moved slowly along the distant highway, but that was all.

"This is the place," Gross said to Kramer. He folded his arms. "Quite a quaint little house."

Kramer said nothing. The two Security Agents behind them were expressionless.

Gross started toward the gate. "Let's go. According to the check he's still alive, but very sick. His mind is agile, however. That seems to be certain. It's said he doesn't leave the house. A woman takes care of his needs. He's very frail."

They went down the stone walk and up onto the porch. Gross rang the bell. They waited. After a time they heard slow footsteps. The door opened. An elderly woman in a shapeless wrapper studied them impassively.

"Security," Gross said, showing his card. "We wish to see Professor Thomas."

"Why?"

"Government business." He glanced at Kramer.

Kramer stepped forward. "I was a pupil of the Professor's," he said. "I'm sure he won't mind seeing us."

The woman hesitated uncertainly. Gross stepped into the doorway. "All right, mother. This is war time. We can't stand out here."

The two Security agents followed him, and Kramer came reluctantly behind, closing the door. Gross stalked down the hall until he came to an open door. He stopped, looking in. Kramer could see the white corner of a bed, a wooden post and the edge of a dresser.

He joined Gross.

In the dark room a withered old man lay, propped up on endless pillows. At first it seemed as if he were asleep; there was no motion or sign of life. But after a time Kramer saw with a faint shock that the old man was watching them intently, his eyes fixed on them, unmoving, unwinking.

"Professor Thomas?" Gross said. "I'm Commander Gross of Security. This man with me is perhaps known to you—"

The faded eyes fixed on Kramer.

"I know him. Philip Kramer…. You've grown heavier, boy." The voice was feeble, the rustle of dry ashes. "Is it true you're married now?"

"Yes. I married Dolores French. You remember her." Kramer came toward the bed. "But we're separated. It didn't work out very well. Our careers—"

"What we came here about, Professor," Gross began, but Kramer cut him off with an impatient wave.

"Let me talk. Can't you and your men get out of here long enough to let me talk to him?"

Gross swallowed. "All right, Kramer." He nodded to the two men. The three of them left the room, going out into the hall and closing the door after them.

The old man in the bed watched Kramer silently. "I don't think much of him," he said at last. "I've seen his type before. What's he want?"

"Nothing. He just came along. Can I sit down?" Kramer found a stiff upright chair beside the bed. "If I'm bothering you—"

"No. I'm glad to see you again, Philip. After so long. I'm sorry your marriage didn't work out."

"How have you been?"

"I've been very ill. I'm afraid that my moment on the world's stage has almost ended." The ancient eyes studied the younger man reflectively. "You look as if you have been doing well. Like everyone else I thought highly of. You've gone to the top in this society."

Kramer smiled. Then he became serious. "Professor, there's a project we're working on that I want to talk to you about. It's the first ray of hope we've had in this whole war. If it works, we may be able to crack the yuk defenses, get some ships into their system. If we can do that the war might be brought to an end."

"Go on. Tell me about it, if you wish."

"It's a long shot, this project. It may not work at all, but we have to give it a try."

"It's obvious that you came here because of it," Professor Thomas murmured. "I'm becoming curious. Go on."

After Kramer finished the old man lay back in the bed without speaking. At last he sighed.

"I understand. A human mind, taken out of a human body." He sat up a little, looking at Kramer. "I suppose you're thinking of me."

Kramer said nothing.

"Before I make my decision I want to see the papers on this, the theory and outline of construction. I'm not sure I like it.—For reasons of my own, I mean. But I want to look at the material. If you'll do that—"

"Certainly." Kramer stood up and went to the door. Gross and the two Security Agents were standing outside, waiting tensely. "Gross, come inside."

They filed into the room.

"Give the Professor the papers," Kramer said. "He wants to study them before deciding."

Gross brought the file out of his coat pocket, a manila envelope. He handed it to the old man on the bed. "Here it is, Professor. You're welcome to examine it. Will you give us your answer as soon as possible? We're very anxious to begin, of course."

"I'll give you my answer when I've decided." He took the envelope with a thin, trembling hand. "My decision depends on what I find out from these papers. If I don't like what I find, then I will not become involved with this work in any shape or form." He opened the envelope with shaking hands. "I'm looking for one thing."

"What is it?" Gross said.

"That's my affair. Leave me a number by which I can reach you when I've decided."

Silently, Gross put his card down on the dresser. As they went out Professor Thomas was already reading the first of the papers, the outline of the theory.

Kramer sat across from Dale Winter, his second in line. "What then?" Winter said.

"He's going to contact us." Kramer scratched with a drawing pen on some paper. "I don't know what to think."

"What do you mean?" Winter's good-natured face was puzzled.

"Look." Kramer stood up, pacing back and forth, his hands in his uniform pockets. "He was my teacher in college. I respected him as a man, as well as a teacher. He was more than a voice, a talking book. He was a person, a calm, kindly person I could look up to. I always wanted to be like him, someday. Now look at me."

"So?"

"Look at what I'm asking. I'm asking for his life, as if he were some kind of laboratory animal kept around in a cage, not a man, a teacher at all."

"Do you think he'll do it?"

"I don't know." Kramer went to the window. He stood looking out. "In a way, I hope not."

"But if he doesn't—"

"Then we'll have to find somebody else. I know. There would be somebody else. Why did Dolores have to—"

The vidphone rang. Kramer pressed the button.

"This is Gross." The heavy features formed. "The old man called me. Professor Thomas."

"What did he say?" He knew; he could tell already, by the sound of Gross' voice.

"He said he'd do it. I was a little surprised myself, but apparently he means it. We've already made arrangements for his admission to the hospital. His lawyer is drawing up the statement of liability."

Kramer only half heard. He nodded wearily. "All right. I'm glad. I suppose we can go ahead, then."

"You don't sound very glad."

"I wonder why he decided to go ahead with it."

"He was very certain about it." Gross sounded pleased. "He called me quite early. I was still in bed. You know, this calls for a celebration."

"Sure," Kramer said. "It sure does."

Toward the middle of August the project neared completion. They stood outside in the hot autumn heat, looking up at the sleek metal sides of the ship.

Gross thumped the metal with his hand. "Well, it won't be long. We can begin the test any time."

"Tell us more about this," an officer in gold braid said. "It's such an unusual concept."

"Is there really a human brain inside the ship?" a dignitary asked, a small man in a rumpled suit. "And the brain is actually alive?"

"Gentlemen, this ship is guided by a living brain instead of the usual Johnson relay-control system. But the brain is not conscious. It will function by reflex only. The practical difference between it and the Johnson system is this: a human brain is far more intricate than any man-made structure, and its ability to adapt itself to a situation, to respond to danger, is far beyond anything that could be artificially built."

Gross paused, cocking his ear. The turbines of the ship were beginning to rumble, shaking the ground under them with a deep vibration. Kramer was standing a short distance away from the others, his arms folded, watching silently. At the sound of the turbines he walked quickly around the ship to the other side. A few workmen were clearing away the last of the waste, the scraps of wiring and scaffolding. They glanced up at him and went on hurriedly with their work. Kramer mounted the ramp and entered the control cabin of the ship. Winter was sitting at the controls with a Pilot from Space-transport.

"How's it look?" Kramer asked.

"All right." Winter got up. "He tells me that it would be best to take off manually. The robot controls—" Winter hesitated. "I mean, the built-in controls, can take over later on in space."

"That's right," the Pilot said. "It's customary with the Johnson system, and so in this case we should—"

"Can you tell anything yet?" Kramer asked.

"No," the Pilot said slowly. "I don't think so. I've been going over everything. It seems to be in good order. There's only one thing I wanted to ask you about." He put his hand on the control board. "There are some changes here I don't understand."

"Changes?"

"Alterations from the original design. I wonder what the purpose is."

Kramer took a set of the plans from his coat. "Let me look." He turned the pages over. The Pilot watched carefully over his shoulder.

"The changes aren't indicated on your copy," the Pilot said. "I wonder—" He stopped. Commander Gross had entered the control cabin.

"Gross, who authorized alterations?" Kramer said. "Some of the wiring has been changed."

"Why, your old friend." Gross signaled to the field tower through the window.

"My old friend?"

"The Professor. He took quite an active interest." Gross turned to the Pilot. "Let's get going. We have to take this out past gravity for the test they tell me. Well, perhaps it's for the best. Are you ready?"

"Sure." The Pilot sat down and moved some of the controls around. "Anytime."

"Go ahead, then," Gross said.

"The Professor—" Kramer began, but at that moment there was a tremendous roar and the ship leaped under him. He grasped one of the wall holds and hung on as best he could. The cabin was filling with a steady throbbing, the raging of the jet turbines underneath them.

The ship leaped. Kramer closed his eyes and held his breath. They were moving out into space, gaining speed each moment.

"Well, what do you think?" Winter said nervously. "Is it time yet?"

"A little longer," Kramer said. He was sitting on the floor of the cabin, down by the control wiring. He had removed the metal covering-plate, exposing the complicated maze of relay wiring. He was studying it, comparing it to the wiring diagrams.

"What's the matter?" Gross said.

"These changes. I can't figure out what they're for. The only pattern I can make out is that for some reason—"

"Let me look," the Pilot said. He squatted down beside Kramer. "You were saying?"

"See this lead here? Originally it was switch controlled. It closed and opened automatically, according to temperature change. Now it's wired so that the central control system operates it. The same with the others. A lot of this was still mechanical, worked by pressure, temperature, stress. Now it's under the central master."

"The brain?" Gross said. "You mean it's been altered so that the brain manipulates it?"

Kramer nodded. "Maybe Professor Thomas felt that no mechanical relays could be trusted. Maybe he thought that things would be happening too fast. But some of these could close in a split second. The brake rockets could go on as quickly as—"

"Hey," Winter said from the control seat. "We're getting near the moon stations. What'll I do?"

They looked out the port. The corroded surface of the moon gleamed up at them, a corrupt and sickening sight. They were moving swiftly toward it.

"I'll take it," the Pilot said. He eased Winter out of the way and strapped himself in place. The ship began to move away from the moon as he manipulated the controls. Down below them they could see the observation stations dotting the surface, and the tiny squares that were the openings of the underground factories and hangars. A red blinker winked up at them and the Pilot's fingers moved on the board in answer.

"We're past the moon," the Pilot said, after a time. The moon had fallen behind them; the ship was heading into outer space. "Well, we can go ahead with it."

Kramer did not answer.

"Mr. Kramer, we can go ahead any time."

Kramer started. "Sorry. I was thinking. All right, thanks." He frowned, deep in thought.

"What is it?" Gross asked.

"The wiring changes. Did you understand the reason for them when you gave the okay to the workmen?"

Gross flushed. "You know I know nothing about technical material. I'm in Security."

"Then you should have consulted me."

"What does it matter?" Gross grinned wryly. "We're going to have to start putting our faith in the old man sooner or later."

The Pilot stepped back from the board. His face was pale and set. "Well, it's done," he said. "That's it."

"What's done?" Kramer said.

"We're on automatic. The brain. I turned the board over to it— to him, I mean. The Old Man." The Pilot lit a cigarette and puffed nervously. "Let's keep our fingers crossed."

The ship was coasting evenly, in the hands of its invisible pilot. Far down inside the ship, carefully armoured and protected, a soft human brain lay in a tank of liquid, a thousand minute electric charges playing over its surface. As the charges rose they were picked up and amplified, fed into relay systems, advanced, carried on through the entire ship—

Gross wiped his forehead nervously. "So he is running it, now. I hope he knows what he's doing."

Kramer nodded enigmatically. "I think he does."

"What do you mean?"

"Nothing." Kramer walked to the port. "I see we're still moving in a straight line." He picked up the microphone. "We can instruct the brain orally, through this." He blew against the microphone experimentally.

"Go on," Winter said.

"Bring the ship around half-right," Kramer said. "Decrease speed."

They waited. Time passed. Gross looked at Kramer. "No change. Nothing."

"Wait."

Slowly, the ship was beginning to turn. The turbines missed, reducing their steady beat. The ship was taking up its new course, adjusting itself. Nearby some space debris rushed past, incinerating in the blasts of the turbine jets.

"So far so good," Gross said.

They began to breathe more easily. The invisible pilot had taken control smoothly, calmly. The ship was in good hands. Kramer spoke a few more words into the microphone, and they swung again. Now they were moving back the way they had come, toward the moon.

"Let's see what he does when we enter the moon's pull," Kramer said. "He was a good mathematician, the old man. He could handle any kind of problem."

The ship veered, turning away from the moon. The great eaten-away globe fell behind them.

Gross breathed a sigh of relief. "That's that."

"One more thing." Kramer picked up the microphone. "Return to the moon and land the ship at the first space field," he said into it.

"Good Lord," Winter murmured. "Why are you—"

"Be quiet." Kramer stood, listening. The turbines gasped and roared as the ship swung full around, gaining speed. They were moving back, back toward the moon again. The ship dipped down, heading toward the great globe below.

"We're going a little fast," the Pilot said. "I don't see how he can put down at this velocity."

The port filled up, as the globe swelled rapidly. The Pilot hurried toward the board, reaching for the controls. All at once the ship jerked. The nose lifted and the ship shot out into space, away from the moon, turning at an oblique angle. The men were thrown to the floor by the sudden change in course. They got to their feet again, speechless, staring at each other.

The Pilot gazed down at the board. "It wasn't me! I didn't touch a thing. I didn't even get to it."

The ship was gaining speed each moment. Kramer hesitated. "Maybe you better switch it back to manual."

The Pilot closed the switch. He took hold of the steering controls and moved them experimentally. "Nothing." He turned around. "Nothing. It doesn't respond."

No one spoke.

"You can see what has happened," Kramer said calmly. "The old man won't let go of it, now that he has it. I was afraid of this when I saw the wiring changes. Everything in this ship is centrally controlled, even the cooling system, the hatches, the garbage release. We're helpless."

"Nonsense." Gross strode to the board. He took hold of the wheel and turned it. The ship continued on its course, moving away from the moon, leaving it behind.

"Release!" Kramer said into the microphone. "Let go of the controls! We'll take it back. Release."

"No good," the Pilot said. "Nothing." He spun the useless wheel. "It's dead, completely dead."

"And we're still heading out," Winter said, grinning foolishly. "We'll be going through the first-line defense belt in a few minutes. If they don't shoot us down—"

"We better radio back." The Pilot clicked the radio to send. "I'll contact the main bases, one of the observation stations."

"Better get the defense belt, at the speed we're going. We'll be into it in a minute."

"And after that," Kramer said, "we'll be in outer space. He's moving us toward outspace velocity. Is this ship equipped with baths?"

"Baths?" Gross said.

"The sleep tanks. For space-drive. We may need them if we go much faster."

"But good God, where are we going?" Gross said. "Where— where's he taking us?"

The Pilot obtained contact. "This is Dwight, on ship," he said. "We're entering the defense zone at high velocity. Don't fire on us."

"Turn back," the impersonal voice came through the speaker. "You're not allowed in the defense zone."

"We can't. We've lost control."

"Lost control?"

"This is an experimental ship."

Gross took the radio. "This is Commander Gross, Security. We're being carried into outer space. There's nothing we can do. Is there any way that we can be removed from this ship?"

A hesitation. "We have some fast pursuit ships that could pick you up if you wanted to jump. The chances are good they'd find you. Do you have space flares?"

"We do," the Pilot said. "Let's try it."

"Abandon ship?" Kramer said. "If we leave now we'll never see it again."

"What else can we do? We're gaining speed all the time. Do you propose that we stay here?"

"No." Kramer shook his head. "Damn it, there ought to be a better solution."

"Could you contact him?" Winter asked. "The Old Man? Try to reason with him?"

"It's worth a chance," Gross said. "Try it."

"All right." Kramer took the microphone. He paused a moment. "Listen! Can you hear me? This is Phil Kramer. Can you hear me, Professor. Can you hear me? I want you to release the controls."

There was silence.

"This is Kramer, Professor. Can you hear me? Do you remember who I am? Do you understand who this is?"

Above the control panel the wall speaker made a sound, a sputtering static. They looked up.

"Can you hear me, Professor. This is Philip Kramer. I want you to give the ship back to us. If you can hear me, release the controls! Let go, Professor. Let go!"

Static. A rushing sound, like the wind. They gazed at each other. There was silence for a moment.

"It's a waste of time," Gross said.

"No—listen!"

The sputter came again. Then, mixed with the sputter, almost lost in it, a voice came, toneless, without inflection, a mechanical, lifeless voice from the metal speaker in the wall, above their heads.

"... Is it you, Philip? I can't make you out. Darkness.... Who's there? With you...."

"It's me, Kramer." His fingers tightened against the microphone handle. "You must release the controls, Professor. We have to get back to Terra. You must."

Silence. Then the faint, faltering voice came again, a little stronger than before. "Kramer. Everything so strange. I was right, though. Consciousness result of thinking. Necessary result. Cognito ergo sum. Retain conceptual ability. Can you hear me?"

"Yes, Professor—"

"I altered the wiring. Control. I was fairly certain…. I wonder if I can do it. Try…."

Suddenly the air-conditioning snapped into operation. It snapped abruptly off again. Down the corridor a door slammed. Something thudded. The men stood listening. Sounds came from all sides of them, switches shutting, opening. The lights blinked off; they were in darkness. The lights came back on, and at the same time the heating coils dimmed and faded.

"Good God!" Winter said.

Water poured down on them, the emergency fire-fighting system. There was a screaming rush of air. One of the escape hatches had slid back, and the air was roaring frantically out into space.

The hatch banged closed. The ship subsided into silence. The heating coils glowed into life. As suddenly as it had begun the weird exhibition ceased.

"I can do—everything," the dry, toneless voice came from the wall speaker. "It is all controlled. Kramer, I wish to talk to you. I've been—been thinking. I haven't seen you in many years. A lot to discuss. You've changed, boy. We have much to discuss. Your wife—"

The Pilot grabbed Kramer's arm. "There's a ship standing off our bow. Look."

They ran to the port. A slender pale craft was moving along with them, keeping pace with them. It was signal-blinking.

"A Terran pursuit ship," the Pilot said. "Let's jump. They'll pick us up. Suits—"

He ran to a supply cupboard and turned the handle. The door opened and he pulled the suits out onto the floor.

"Hurry," Gross said. A panic seized them. They dressed frantically, pulling the heavy garments over them. Winter staggered to the escape hatch and stood by it, waiting for the others. They joined him, one by one.

"Let's go!" Gross said. "Open the hatch."

Winter tugged at the hatch. "Help me."

They grabbed hold, tugging together. Nothing happened. The hatch refused to budge.

"Get a crowbar," the Pilot said.

"Hasn't anyone got a blaster?" Gross looked frantically around. "Damn it, blast it open!"

"Pull," Kramer grated. "Pull together."

"Are you at the hatch?" the toneless voice came, drifting and eddying through the corridors of the ship. They looked up, staring around them. "I sense something nearby, outside. A ship? You are leaving, all of you? Kramer, you are leaving, too? Very unfortunate. I had hoped we could talk. Perhaps at some other time you might be induced to remain."

"Open the hatch!" Kramer said, staring up at the impersonal walls of the ship. "For God's sake, open it!"

There was silence, an endless pause. Then, very slowly, the hatch slid back. The air screamed out, rushing past them into space.

One by one they leaped, one after the other, propelled away by the repulsive material of the suits. A few minutes later they were being hauled aboard the pursuit ship. As the last one of them was lifted through the port, their own ship pointed itself suddenly upward and shot off at tremendous speed. It disappeared.

Kramer removed his helmet, gasping. Two sailors held onto him and began to wrap him in blankets. Gross sipped a mug of coffee, shivering.

"It's gone," Kramer murmured.

"I'll have an alarm sent out," Gross said.

"What's happened to your ship?" a sailor asked curiously. "It sure took off in a hurry. Who's on it?"

"We'll have to have it destroyed," Gross went on, his face grim. "It's got to be destroyed. There's no telling what it—what he has in mind." Gross sat down weakly on a metal bench. "What a close call for us. We were so damn trusting."

"What could he be planning," Kramer said, half to himself. "It doesn't make sense. I don't get it."

As the ship sped back toward the moon base they sat around the table in the dining room, sipping hot coffee and thinking, not saying very much.

"Look here," Gross said at last. "What kind of man was Professor Thomas? What do you remember about him?"

Kramer put his coffee mug down. "It was ten years ago. I don't remember much. It's vague."

He let his mind run back over the years. He and Dolores had been at Hunt College together, in physics and the life sciences. The College was small and set back away from the momentum of modern life. He had gone there because it was his home town, and his father had gone there before him.

Professor Thomas had been at the College a long time, as long as anyone could remember. He was a strange old man, keeping to himself most of the time. There were many things that he disapproved of, but he seldom said what they were.

"Do you recall anything that might help us?" Gross asked. "Anything that would give us a clue as to what he might have in mind?"

Kramer nodded slowly. "I remember one thing...."

One day he and the Professor had been sitting together in the school chapel, talking leisurely.

"Well, you'll be out of school, soon," the Professor had said. "What are you going to do?"

"Do? Work at one of the Government Research Projects, I suppose."

"And eventually? What's your ultimate goal?"

Kramer had smiled. "The question is unscientific. It presupposes such things as ultimate ends."

"Suppose instead along these lines, then: What if there were no war and no Government Research Projects? What would you do, then?"

"I don't know. But how can I imagine a hypothetical situation like that? There's been war as long as I can remember. We're geared for war. I don't know what I'd do. I suppose I'd adjust, get used to it."

The Professor had stared at him. "Oh, you do think you'd get accustomed to it, eh? Well, I'm glad of that. And you think you could find something to do?"

Gross listened intently. "What do you infer from this, Kramer?"

"Not much. Except that he was against war."

"We're all against war," Gross pointed out.

"True. But he was withdrawn, set apart. He lived very simply, cooking his own meals. His wife died many years ago. He was born in Europe, in Italy. He changed his name when he came to the United States. He used to read Dante and Milton. He even had a Bible."

"Very anachronistic, don't you think?"

"Yes, he lived quite a lot in the past. He found an old phonograph and records, and he listened to the old music. You saw his house, how old-fashioned it was."

"Did he have a file?" Winter asked Gross.

"With Security? No, none at all. As far as we could tell he never engaged in political work, never joined anything or even seemed to have strong political convictions."

"No," Kramer, agreed. "About all he ever did was walk through the hills. He liked nature."

"Nature can be of great use to a scientist," Gross said. "There wouldn't be any science without it."

"Kramer, what do you think his plan is, taking control of the ship and disappearing?" Winter said.

"Maybe the transfer made him insane," the Pilot said. "Maybe there's no plan, nothing rational at all."

"But he had the ship rewired, and he had made sure that he would retain consciousness and memory before he even agreed to the operation. He must have had something planned from the start. But what?"

"Perhaps he just wanted to stay alive longer," Kramer said. "He was old and about to die. Or—"

"Or what?"

"Nothing." Kramer stood up. "I think as soon as we get to the moon base I'll make a vidcall to earth. I want to talk to somebody about this."

"Who's that?" Gross asked.

"Dolores. Maybe she remembers something."

"That's a good idea," Gross said.

"Where are you calling from?" Dolores asked, when he succeeded in reaching her.

"From the moon base."

"All kinds of rumors are running around. Why didn't the ship come back? What happened?"

"I'm afraid he ran off with it."

"He?"

"The Old Man. Professor Thomas." Kramer explained what had happened.

Dolores listened intently. "How strange. And you think he planned it all in advance, from the start?"

"I'm certain. He asked for the plans of construction and the theoretical diagrams at once."

"But why? What for?"

"I don't know. Look, Dolores. What do you remember about him? Is there anything that might give a clue to all this?"

"Like what?"

"I don't know. That's the trouble."

On the vidscreen Dolores knitted her brow. "I remember he raised chickens in his back yard, and once he had a goat." She smiled. "Do you remember the day the goat got loose and wandered down the main street of town? Nobody could figure out where it came from."

"Anything else?"

"No." He watched her struggling, trying to remember. "He wanted to have a farm, sometime, I know."

"All right. Thanks." Kramer touched the switch. "When I get back to Terra maybe I'll stop and see you."

"Let me know how it works out."

He cut the line and the picture dimmed and faded. He walked slowly back to where Gross and some officers of the Military were sitting at a chart table, talking.

"Any luck?" Gross said, looking up.

"No. All she remembers is that he kept a goat."

"Come over and look at this detail chart." Gross motioned him around to his side. "Watch!"

Kramer saw the record tabs moving furiously, the little white dots racing back and forth.

"What's happening?" he asked.

"A squadron outside the defense zone has finally managed to contact the ship. They're maneuvering now, for position. Watch."

The white counters were forming a barrel formation around a black dot that was moving steadily across the board, away from the central position. As they watched, the white dots constricted around it.

"They're ready to open fire," a technician at the board said. "Commander, what shall we tell them to do?"

Gross hesitated. "I hate to be the one who makes the decision. When it comes right down to it—"

"It's not just a ship," Kramer said. "It's a man, a living person. A human being is up there, moving through space. I wish we knew what—"

"But the order has to be given. We can't take any chances. Suppose he went over to them, to the yuks."

Kramer's jaw dropped. "My God, he wouldn't do that."

"Are you sure? Do you know what he'll do?"

"He wouldn't do that."

Gross turned to the technician. "Tell them to go ahead."

"I'm sorry, sir, but now the ship has gotten away. Look down at the board."

Gross stared down, Kramer over his shoulder. The black dot had slipped through the white dots and had moved off at an abrupt angle. The white dots were broken up, dispersing in confusion.

"He's an unusual strategist," one of the officers said. He traced the line. "It's an ancient maneuver, an old Prussian device, but it worked."

The white dots were turning back. "Too many yuk ships out that far," Gross said. "Well, that's what you get when you don't act quickly." He looked up coldly at Kramer. "We should have done it when we had him. Look at him go!" He jabbed a finger at the rapidly moving black dot. The dot came to the edge of the board and stopped. It had reached the limit of the chartered area. "See?"

—Now what? Kramer thought, watching. So the Old Man had escaped the cruisers and gotten away. He was alert, all right; there was nothing wrong with his mind. Or with his ability to control his new body.

Body—The ship was a new body for him. He had traded in the old dying body, withered and frail, for this hulking frame of metal and plastic, turbines and rocket jets. He was strong, now. Strong and big. The new body was more powerful than a thousand human bodies. But how long would it last him? The average life of a cruiser was only ten years. With careful handling he might get twenty out of it, before some essential part failed and there was no way to replace it.

And then, what then? What would he do, when something failed and there was no one to fix it for him? That would be the end. Someplace, far out in the cold darkness of space, the ship would slow down, silent and lifeless, to exhaust its last heat into the eternal timelessness of outer space. Or perhaps it would crash on some barren asteroid, burst into a million fragments.

It was only a question of time.

"Your wife didn't remember anything?" Gross said.

"I told you. Only that he kept a goat, once."

"A hell of a lot of help that is."

Kramer shrugged. "It's not my fault."

"I wonder if we'll ever see him again." Gross stared down at the indicator dot, still hanging at the edge of the board. "I wonder if he'll ever move back this way."

"I wonder, too," Kramer said.

That night Kramer lay in bed, tossing from side to side, unable to sleep. The moon gravity, even artificially increased, was unfamiliar to him and it made him uncomfortable. A thousand thoughts wandered loose in his head as he lay, fully awake.

What did it all mean? What was the Professor's plan? Maybe they would never know. Maybe the ship was gone for good; the Old Man had left forever, shooting into outer space. They might never find out why he had done it, what purpose—if any—had been in his mind.

Kramer sat up in bed. He turned on the light and lit a cigarette. His quarters were small, a metal-lined bunk room, part of the moon station base.

The Old Man had wanted to talk to him. He had wanted to discuss things, hold a conversation, but in the hysteria and confusion all they had been able to think of was getting away. The ship was rushing off with them, carrying them into outer space. Kramer set his jaw. Could they be blamed for jumping? They had no idea where they were being taken, or why. They were helpless, caught in their own ship, and the pursuit ship standing by waiting to pick them up was their only chance. Another half hour and it would have been too late.

But what had the Old Man wanted to say? What had he intended to tell him, in those first confusing moments when the ship around them had come alive, each metal strut and wire suddenly animate, the body of a living creature, a vast metal organism?

It was weird, unnerving. He could not forget it, even now. He looked around the small room uneasily. What did it signify, the coming to life of metal and plastic? All at once they had found themselves inside a living creature, in its stomach, like Jonah inside the whale.

It had been alive, and it had talked to them, talked calmly and rationally, as it rushed them off, faster and faster into outer space. The wall speaker and circuit had become the vocal cords and mouth, the wiring the spinal cord and nerves, the hatches and relays and circuit breakers the muscles.

They had been helpless, completely helpless. The ship had, in a brief second, stolen their power away from them and left them defenseless, practically at its mercy. It was not right; it made him uneasy. All his life he had controlled machines, bent nature and the forces of nature to man and man's needs. The human race had slowly evolved until it was in a position to operate things, run them as it saw fit. Now all at once it had been plunged back down the ladder again, prostrate before a Power against which they were children.

Kramer got out of bed. He put on his bathrobe and began to search for a cigarette. While he was searching, the vidphone rang.

He snapped the vidphone on.

"Yes?"

The face of the immediate monitor appeared. "A call from Terra, Mr. Kramer. An emergency call."

"Emergency call? For me? Put it through." Kramer came awake, brushing his hair back out of his eyes. Alarm plucked at him.

From the speaker a strange voice came. "Philip Kramer? Is this Kramer?"

"Yes. Go on."

"This is General Hospital, New York City, Terra. Mr. Kramer, your wife is here. She has been critically injured in an accident. Your name was given to us to call. Is it possible for you to—"

"How badly?" Kramer gripped the vidphone stand. "Is it serious?"

"Yes, it's serious, Mr. Kramer. Are you able to come here? The quicker you can come the better."

"Yes." Kramer nodded. "I'll come. Thanks."

The screen died as the connection was broken. Kramer waited a moment. Then he tapped the button. The screen relit again. "Yes, sir," the monitor said.

"Can I get a ship to Terra at once? It's an emergency. My wife—"

"There's no ship leaving the moon for eight hours. You'll have to wait until the next period."

"Isn't there anything I can do?"

"We can broadcast a general request to all ships passing through this area. Sometimes cruisers pass by here returning to Terra for repairs."

"Will you broadcast that for me? I'll come down to the field."

"Yes sir. But there may be no ship in the area for awhile. It's a gamble." The screen died.

Kramer dressed quickly. He put on his coat and hurried to the lift. A moment later he was running across the general receiving lobby, past the rows of vacant desks and conference tables. At the door the sentries stepped aside and he went outside, onto the great concrete steps.

The face of the moon was in shadow. Below him the field stretched out in total darkness, a black void, endless, without form. He made his way carefully down the steps and along the ramp along the side of the field, to the control tower. A faint row of red lights showed him the way.

Two soldiers challenged him at the foot of the tower, standing in the shadows, their guns ready.

"Kramer?"

"Yes." A light was flashed in his face.

"Your call has been sent out already."

"Any luck?" Kramer asked.

"There's a cruiser nearby that has made contact with us. It has an injured jet and is moving slowly back toward Terra, away from the line."

"Good." Kramer nodded, a flood of relief rushing through him. He lit a cigarette and gave one to each of the soldiers. The soldiers lit up.

"Sir," one of them asked, "is it true about the experimental ship?"

"What do you mean?"

"It came to life and ran off?"

"No, not exactly," Kramer said. "It had a new type of control system instead of the Johnson units. It wasn't properly tested."

"But sir, one of the cruisers that was there got up close to it, and a buddy of mine says this ship acted funny. He never saw anything like it. It was like when he was fishing once on Terra, in Washington State, fishing for bass. The fish were smart, going this way and that—"

"Here's your cruiser," the other soldier said. "Look!"

An enormous vague shape was setting slowly down onto the field. They could make nothing out but its row of tiny green blinkers. Kramer stared at the shape.

"Better hurry, sir," the soldiers said. "They don't stick around here very long."

"Thanks." Kramer loped across the field, toward the black shape that rose up above him, extended across the width of the field. The ramp was down from the side of the cruiser and he caught hold of it. The ramp rose, and a moment later Kramer was inside the hold of the ship. The hatch slid shut behind him.

As he made his way up the stairs to the main deck the turbines roared up from the moon, out into space.

Kramer opened the door to the main deck. He stopped suddenly, staring around him in surprise. There was nobody in sight. The ship was deserted.

"Good God," he said. Realization swept over him, numbing him. He sat down on a bench, his head swimming. "Good God."

The ship roared out into space leaving the moon and Terra farther behind each moment.

And there was nothing he could do.

"So it was you who put the call through," he said at last. "It was you who called me on the vidphone, not any hospital on Terra. It was all part of the plan." He looked up and around him. "And Dolores is really—"

"Your wife is fine," the wall speaker above him said tonelessly. "It was a fraud. I am sorry to trick you that way, Philip, but it was all I could think of. Another day and you would have been back on Terra. I don't want to remain in this area any longer than necessary. They have been so certain of finding me out in deep space that I have been able to stay here without too much danger. But even the purloined letter was found eventually."

Kramer smoked his cigarette nervously. "What are you going to do? Where are we going?"

"First, I want to talk to you. I have many things to discuss. I was very disappointed when you left me, along with the others. I had hoped that you would remain." The dry voice chuckled. "Remember how we used to talk in the old days, you and I? That was a long time ago."

The ship was gaining speed. It plunged through space at tremendous speed, rushing through the last of the defense zone and out beyond. A rush of nausea made Kramer bend over for a moment.

When he straightened up the voice from the wall went on, "I'm sorry to step it up so quickly, but we are still in danger. Another few moments and we'll be free."

"How about yuk ships? Aren't they out here?"

"I've already slipped away from several of them. They're quite curious about me."

"Curious?"

"They sense that I'm different, more like their own organic mines. They don't like it. I believe they will begin to withdraw from this area, soon. Apparently they don't want to get involved with me. They're an odd race, Philip. I would have liked to study them closely, try to learn something about them. I'm of the opinion that they use no inert material. All their equipment and instruments are alive, in some form or other. They don't construct or build at all.

The idea of making is foreign to them. They utilize existing forms. Even their ships—"

"Where are we going?" Kramer said. "I want to know where you are taking me."

"Frankly, I'm not certain."

"You're not certain?"

"I haven't worked some details out. There are a few vague spots in my program, still. But I think that in a short while I'll have them ironed out."

"What is your program?" Kramer said.

"It's really very simple. But don't you want to come into the control room and sit? The seats are much more comfortable than that metal bench."

Kramer went into the control room and sat down at the control board. Looking at the useless apparatus made him feel strange.

"What's the matter?" the speaker above the board rasped.

Kramer gestured helplessly. "I'm—powerless. I can't do anything. And I don't like it. Do you blame me?"

"No. No, I don't blame you. But you'll get your control back, soon. Don't worry. This is only a temporary expedient, taking you off this way. It was something I didn't contemplate. I forgot that orders would be given out to shoot me on sight."

"It was Gross' idea."

"I don't doubt that. My conception, my plan, came to me as soon as you began to describe your project, that day at my house. I saw at once that you were wrong; you people have no understanding of the mind at all. I realized that the transfer of a human brain from an organic body to a complex artificial space ship would not involve the loss of the intellectualization faculty of the mind. When a man thinks, he is.

"When I realized that, I saw the possibility of an age-old dream becoming real. I was quite elderly when I first met you, Philip. Even then my life-span had come pretty much to its end. I could look ahead to nothing but death, and with it the extinction of all my ideas. I had made no mark on the world, none at all. My students, one by one, passed from me into the world, to take up jobs in the great Research Project, the search for better and bigger weapons of war.

"The world has been fighting for a long time, first with itself, then with the Martians, then with these beings from Proxima Centauri, whom we know nothing about. The human society has evolved war as a cultural institution, like the science of astronomy, or mathematics. War is a part of our lives, a career, a respected vocation. Bright, alert young men and women move into it, putting their shoulders to the wheel as they did in the time of Nebuchadnezzar. It has always been so.

"But is it innate in mankind? I don't think so. No social custom is innate. There were many human groups that did not go to war; the Eskimos never grasped the idea at all, and the American Indians never took to it well.

"But these dissenters were wiped out, and a cultural pattern was established that became the standard for the whole planet. Now it has become ingrained in us.

"But if someplace along the line some other way of settling problems had arisen and taken hold, something different than the massing of men and material to—"

"What's your plan?" Kramer said. "I know the theory. It was part of one of your lectures."

"Yes, buried in a lecture on plant selection, as I recall. When you came to me with this proposition I realized that perhaps my conception could be brought to life, after all. If my theory were right that war is only a habit, not an instinct, a society built up apart from Terra with a minimum of cultural roots might develop differently. If it failed to absorb our outlook, if it could start out on another foot, it might not arrive at the same point to which we have come: a dead end, with nothing but greater and greater wars in sight, until nothing is left but ruin and destruction everywhere.

"Of course, there would have to be a Watcher to guide the experiment, at first. A crisis would undoubtedly come very quickly, probably in the second generation. Cain would arise almost at once.

"You see, Kramer, I estimate that if I remain at rest most of the time, on some small planet or moon, I may be able to keep functioning for almost a hundred years. That would be time enough, sufficient to see the direction of the new colony. After that—Well, after that it would be up to the colony itself.

"Which is just as well, of course. Man must take control eventually, on his own. One hundred years, and after that they will have control of their own destiny. Perhaps I am wrong, perhaps war is more than a habit. Perhaps it is a law of the universe, that things can only survive as groups by group violence.

"But I'm going ahead and taking the chance that it is only a habit, that I'm right, that war is something we're so accustomed to that we don't realize it is a very unnatural thing. Now as to the place! I'm still a little vague about that. We must find the place, still.

"That's what we're doing now. You and I are going to inspect a few systems off the beaten path, planets where the trading prospects are low enough to keep Terran ships away. I know of one planet that might be a good place. It was reported by the Fairchild Expedition in their original manual. We may look into that, for a start."

The ship was silent.

Kramer sat for a time, staring down at the metal floor under him. The floor throbbed dully with the motion of the turbines. At last he looked up.

"You might be right. Maybe our outlook is only a habit." Kramer got to his feet. "But I wonder if something has occurred to you?"

"What is that?"

"If it's such a deeply ingrained habit, going back thousands of years, how are you going to get your colonists to make the break, leave Terra and Terran customs? How about this generation, the first ones, the people who found the colony? I think you're probably right that the next generation would be free of all this, if there were an—" He grinned. "—An Old Man Above to teach them something else instead."

Kramer looked up at the wall speaker. "How are you going to get the people to leave Terra and come with you, if by your own theory, this generation can't be saved, it all has to start with the next?"

The wall speaker was silent. Then it made a sound, the faint dry chuckle.

"I'm surprised at you, Philip. Settlers can be found. We won't need many, just a few." The speaker chuckled again. "I'll acquaint you with my solution."

At the far end of the corridor a door slid open. There was sound, a hesitant sound. Kramer turned.

"Dolores!"

Dolores Kramer stood uncertainly, looking into the control room. She blinked in amazement. "Phil! What are you doing here? What's going on?"

They stared at each other.

"What's happening?" Dolores said. "I received a vidcall that you had been hurt in a lunar explosion—"

The wall speaker rasped into life. "You see, Philip, that problem is already solved. We don't really need so many people; even a single couple might do."

Kramer nodded slowly. "I see," he murmured thickly. "Just one couple. One man and woman."

"They might make it all right, if there were someone to watch and see that things went as they should. There will be quite a few things I can help you with, Philip. Quite a few. We'll get along very well, I think."

Kramer grinned wryly. "You could even help us name the animals," he said. "I understand that's the first step."

"I'll be glad to," the toneless, impersonal voice said. "As I recall, my part will be to bring them to you, one by one. Then you can do the actual naming."

"I don't understand," Dolores faltered. "What does he mean, Phil? Naming animals. What kind of animals? Where are we going?"

Kramer walked slowly over to the port and stood staring silently out, his arms folded. Beyond the ship a myriad fragments of light gleamed, countless coals glowing in the dark void. Stars, suns, systems. Endless, without number. A universe of worlds. An infinity of planets, waiting for them, gleaming and winking from the darkness.

He turned back, away from the port. "Where are we going?" He smiled at his wife, standing nervous and frightened, her large eyes full of alarm. "I don't know where we are going," he said. "But somehow that doesn't seem too important right now.... I'm beginning to see the Professor's point, it's the result that counts."

And for the first time in many months he put his arm around Dolores. At first she stiffened, the fright and nervousness still in her eyes. But then suddenly she relaxed against him and there were tears wetting her cheeks.

"Phil ... do you really think we can start over again—you and I?"

He kissed her tenderly, then passionately.

And the spaceship shot swiftly through the endless, trackless eternity of the void....

How Deep the Grooves

By PHILIP JOSE FARMER

Until James Carroad performed his experiment, there was one voice inside of each of us that always told the truth.
But after Cervus III, there were suddenly two voices. And only one was the voice of conscience.

ALWAYS in control of himself, Doctor James Carroad lowered his voice.

He said, "You will submit to this test. We must impress the Secretary. The fact that we're willing to use our own unborn baby in the experiment will make that impression a deeper one."

Doctor Jane Carroad, his wife, looked up from the chair in which she sat. Her gaze swept over the tall lean figure in the white scientist's uniform and the two rows of resplendent ribbons and medals on his left chest. She glared into the eyes of her husband.

Scornfully, she said, "You did not want this baby. I did, though now I wonder why. Perhaps, because I wanted to be a mother, no matter what the price. Not to give the State another citizen. But, now we're going to have it, you want to exploit it even before it's born, just as..."

Harshly, he said, "Don't you know what such talk can lead to?"

"Don't worry! I won't tell anyone you didn't desire to add to the State. Nor will I tell anybody how I induced you to have it!"

His face became red, and he said, "You will never again mention that to me! Never again! Understand?"

Jane's neck muscles trembled, but her face was composed. She said, "I'll speak of that, to you, whenever I feel like it. Though, God knows, I'm thoroughly ashamed of it. But I do get a certain sour satisfaction out of knowing that, once in my life, I managed to break down that rigid self-control. I made you act like a normal man, one able to forget himself in his passion for a woman. Doctor Carroad, the great scientist of the State, really forgot himself then."

She gave a short brittle laugh and then settled back in the chair as if she would no longer discuss the matter.

But he would not, could not, let her have the last word. He said, "I only wanted to see how it felt to throw off all restraints. That was all—an experiment. I didn't care for it; it was disgusting. It'll never happen again."

He looked at his wristwatch and said, "Let's go. We must not make the Secretary wait."

She rose slowly, as if the eight months' burden was at last beginning to drain her strength.

"All right. But I'm submitting our baby to this experiment only under protest. If anything happens to it, a potential citizen."

He spun around. "A written protest?"

"I've already sent it in."

"You little fool! Do you want to wreck everything I've worked for?"

Tears filled her eyes.

"James! Does the possible harm to our baby mean nothing to you? Only the medals, the promotions, the power?"

"Nonsense! There's no danger! If there were, wouldn't I know it? Come along now!"

But she did not follow him through the door. Instead, she stood with her face against the wall, her shoulders shaking.

A MOMENT later, Jason Cramer entered. The young man closed the door behind him and put his arm around her. Without protest, she turned and buried her face in his chest. For a while, she could not talk but could only weep.

Finally, she released herself from his embrace and said, "Why is it, Jason, that every time I need a man to cry against, James is not with me but you are?"

"Because he is the one who makes you cry," he said. "And I love you."

"And James," she said, "loves only himself."

"You didn't give me the proper response, Jane. I said I loved you."

She kissed him, though lightly, and murmured, "I think I love you. But I'm not allowed to. Please forget what I said. I mean it."

She walked away from him. Jason Cramer, after making sure that he had no lipstick on his face or uniform, followed her.

Entering the laboratory, Jane Carroad ignored her husband's glare and sat down in the chair in the middle of the room. Immediately thereafter, the Secretary of Science and two Security bodyguards entered.

The Secretary was a stocky dark man of about fifty. He had very thick black eyebrows that looked like pieces of fur pasted above his eyes. He radiated the assurance that he was master, in control of all in the room. Yet, he did not, as was nervously expected by James Carroad and Jason Cramer, take offense because Jane did not rise from the chair to greet him. He gave her a smile, patted her hand, and said, "Is it true you will bear a male baby?"

"That is what the tests indicate," she said.

"Good. Another valuable citizen. A scientist, perhaps. With its genetic background..."

Annoyed because his wife had occupied the center of the stage for too long, Doctor James Carroad loudly cleared his throat. He said, "Citizens, honored Secretary, I've asked you here for a demonstration because I believe that what I have to show you is of utmost importance to the State's future. I have here the secret of what constitutes a good, or bad, citizen of the State."

He paused for effect, which he was getting, and then continued, "As you know, I—and my associates, of course—have perfected an infallible and swift method whereby an enemy spy or deviationist citizen may be unmasked. This method has been in use for three years. During that time, it has exposed many thousands as espionage agents, as traitors, as potential traitors."

The Secretary looked interested. He also looked at his wristwatch. Doctor Carroad refused to notice; he talked on at the same pace. He could justify any amount of time he took, and he intended to use as much as possible.

My Department of Electro-encephalographic Research first produced the devices delicate enough to detect the so-called rho waves emanated by the human brain. The rho or semantic waves. After ten years of hard work, I correlated the action of the rho waves in a particular human brain with the action of the individual's voice mechanisms. That meant, of course, that we had a device which mankind has long dreamed of. A—pardon the term—mind-reading machine."

Carroad purposely avoided scientific terminology. The Secretary did have a Ph.D. in political science, but he knew very little of any biological science.

Jason Cramer, at a snap of the fingers by Carroad, wheeled a large round shining machine to a spot about two feet in front of Jane. It resembled a weird metallic antelope, for it had a long flexible neck at the end of which was an oval and eyeless head with two prongs like horns. These pointed at Jane's skull. On the side of the machine—Cervus III—was a round glass tube. The oscilloscope.

Carroad said, "We no longer have to attach electrodes to the subject's head. We've made that method obsolete. Cervus' prongs pick up rho waves without direct contact. It is also able to cut out 99.99% of the 'noise' that had hampered us in previous research."

Yes, thought Jane, and why don't you tell them that it was Jason Cramer who made that possible, instead of allowing them to think it was you?

At that moment, she reached the peak of her hate for him. She wished that the swelling sleeper within her was not Carroad's but Cramer's. And, wishing that, she knew that she must be falling in love with Cramer.

Carroad's voice slashed into her thoughts.

"And so, using the detected rho waves, which can be matched against definite objective words, we get a verbal picture of what is going in the subject's mind at the conscious level."

He gave an order to Cramer, and Cramer twisted a dial on the small control board on the side of Cervus.

"The machine is now set for semantic relations," Carroad said.

"Jane!" he added so sharply that she was startled. "Repeat this sentence after me! Silently!"

He then gave her a much-quoted phrase from one of the speeches of the Secretary himself. She repressed her scorn of him because of his flattery and dutifully concentrated on thinking the phrase. At the same time, she was aware that her tongue was moving in a noiseless lockstep with the thoughts.

The round tube on the side of Cervus glowed and then began flashing with many twisting threads of light.

"The trained eye," said Carroad, "can interpret those waveforms. But we have a surprise for you to whom the patterns are meaningless. We have perfected a means whereby a technician with a minimum of training may operate Cervus."

HE snapped his fingers. Cramer shot him a look; his face was expressionless, but Jane knew that Cramer resented Carroad's arrogance.

Nevertheless, Cramer obeyed; he adjusted a dial, pushed down on a toggle switch, rotated another dial.

A voice, tonelessly and tinnily mechanical, issued from a loudspeaker beneath the tube. It repeated the phrase that Carroad had given and that Jane was thinking. It continued the repetition until Cramer, at another fingersnap from Carroad, flicked the toggle switch upward.

"As you have just heard," said Carroad triumphantly, "we have converted the waveforms into audible representations of what the subject is thinking."

The Secretary's brows rose like two caterpillars facing each other, and he said, "Very impressive."

But he managed to give the impression that he was thinking. Is that all?

Carroad smiled. He said, "I have much more. Something that, I'm sure, will please you very much. Now, as you know, this machine—my Cervus—is exposing hundreds of deviationists and enemy agents every year.

"Yet, this is *nothing!*"

He stared fiercely at them, but he had a slight smile on the corners of his lips. Jane, knowing him so well, could feel the radiance of his pride at the fact that the Secretary was leaning forward and his mouth was open.

"I say this is nothing! Catching traitors after they have become deviationist is locking the garage after the car has been stolen. What if we had a system of control whereby our citizens would be *unable* to be anything but unquestioningly loyal to the State?"

The Secretary said, "Aah!"

190

"I knew you would be far from indifferent," said Carroad.

CARROAD pointed a finger downwards. Cramer, slowly, his jaws set, twisted the flexible neck of Cervus so that the pronged head pointed directly at Jane's distended stomach. He adjusted controls on the board. Immediately the oscilloscope danced with many intricate figures that were so different from the previous forms that even the untutored eyes of the Secretary could perceive the change.

"Citizens," said Carroad, "for some time after we'd discovered the rho waves in the adult and infant, we searched for their presence in the brain of the unborn child. We had no success for a long time. But that was not because the rho waves did not exist in the embryo. No, it was because we did not have delicate enough instruments. However, a few weeks ago, we succeeded in building one. I experimented upon my unborn child, and I detected weak traces of the rho waves. Thus, I demonstrated that the ability to form words is present, though in undeveloped form, even in the eight-month embryo.

"You're probably wondering what this means. This knowledge does not enable us to make the infant or the unborn speak any sooner. True. But what it does allow us to do is..."

Jane, who had been getting more tense with every word, became rigid. Would he allow this to be done to his own son, his own flesh and blood? Would he permit his child to become a half-robot, an obedient slave to the State, incapable in certain fields of wielding the power of free will? The factor that most marked men from the beasts and the machine?

Numbly, she knew he would.

"...to probe well-defined areas in the undeveloped mind and there to stamp into it certain inhibitory paths. These inhibitions, preconditioned reflexes, as it were, will not, of course, take effect until the child has learned a language. And developed the concepts of citizen and State.

"But, once that is done, the correlation between the semantic waves and the inhibitions is such that the subject is unable to harbor any doubts about the teachings of the State. Or those who interpret the will of the State for its citizens.

"It is not necessary to perform any direct or physical surgery upon the unborn. The reflexes will be installed by Cervus III within a few minutes. As you see, Cervus cannot only receive; it can also transmit. Place a recording inside that receptacle beneath the speaker, actuate it, and, in a short time, you have traced in the grooves of the brain—if you will pardon an unscientific comparison—the voice of the State."

There was a silence. Jane and Cramer were unsuccessful in hiding their repulsion, but the others did not notice them. The Secretary and his bodyguards were staring at Carroad.

AFTER several minutes, the Secretary broke the silence; "Doctor Carroad, are you sure that this treatment will not harm the creative abilities of the child? After all, we might make a first-class citizen, in the political sense, out of your child. Yet, we might wreck his potentialities as a first-class scientist. If we do that to our children, we lose out in the technological race. Not to mention the military. We need great generals, too."

"Absolutely not!" replied Carroad, so loudly and flatly that the Secretary was taken aback. "My computations, rechecked at least a dozen times, show there is no danger whatsoever. The only part of the brain affected, a very small area, has nothing to do with the creative functions. To convince you, I am going to perform the first operation upon my own son. Surely, I could do nothing more persuasive than that."

"Yes," said the Secretary, stroking his massive chin. "By the way, can this be done also to the adult?"

"Unfortunately, no," said Carroad.

"Then, we will have to wait a number of years to determine if your theory is correct. And, if we go ahead on the assumption that the theory is correct, and treat every unborn child in the country, we will have spent a tremendous amount of money and time. If you are not correct..."

"I can't be wrong!" said Carroad. His face began to flush, and he shook. Then, suddenly, his face was its normal color, and he was smiling.

Always in control, thought Jane. *Of himself and, if circumstances would allow, of everybody.*

"We don't have to build any extra machines," said Carroad. "A certain amount will be built, anyway, to detect traitors and enemies. These can be used in hospitals, when not in use elsewhere, to condition the unborn. Wait. I will show you how simple, inexpensive, and swift the operation is."

He gestured to Cramer. Cramer, the muscles twitching at the corners of his mouth, looked at Jane. His eyes tried desperately to tell her that he had to obey Carroad's orders. But, if he did, would he be understood, would he be forgiven?

Jane could only sit in the chair with a face as smooth and unmoving as a robot's and allow him to decide for himself without one sign of dissent or consent from her. What, after all, could either do unless they wished to die?

Cramer adjusted the controls.

Even though Jane knew she would feel nothing, she trembled as if a fist were poised to strike.

BRIGHT peaks and valleys danced on the face of the oscilloscope. Carroad, watching them, gave orders to Cramer to move the prongs in minute spirals. When he had located the area he wished, he told Cramer to stop.

"We have just located the exact chain of neurons which are to be altered. You will hear nothing from the speaker because the embryo, of course, has no language. However, to show you some slight portion of Cervus' capabilities, Cramer will stimulate the area responsible for the rho waves before we begin the so-called inhibiting. Watch the scope. You'll see the waves go from a regular pulse into a wild dance."

The cyclopean eye of the oscilloscope became a field of crazed lines, leaping like a horde of barefooted and wire-thin fakirs on a bed of hot coals.

And a voice boomed out, *"Nu'sey! Nu'sey! Wanna d'ink!"*

Jane cried out, "God, what was that?"

The Secretary was startled; Cramer's face paled; Carroad was frozen.

But he recovered quickly, and he spoke sharply. "Cramer, you must have shifted the prongs so they picked up Jane's thoughts."

"I—I never touched them."

"Those were not my thoughts," said Jane.

"Something's wrong," said Carroad, needlessly. "Here. I'll do the adjusting."

He bent the prongs a fraction, checked the controls, and then turned the power on again.

The mechanical voice of Cervus spoke again.

"What do you mean? What're you saying? My father is not crazy! He's a great scientist, a hero of the State. What do you mean? Not any more?"

The Secretary leaped up from the chair and shouted above Cervus' voice, "What is this?"

Carroad turned the machine off and said, "I—I don't know."

Jane had never seen him so shaken.

"Well, find out! That's your business!"

Carroad's hand shook; one eye began to twitch. But he bent again to the adjustment of the dials. He directed the exceedingly narrow beam along the area from which the semantic waves originated. Only a high-pitched gabble emerged from the speaker, for Carroad had increased the speed. It was as if he were afraid to hear the normal rate of speech.

Jane's eyes began to widen. A thought was dawning palely, but horribly, on the horizon of her mind. If, by some intuition, she was just beginning to see the truth... But no, that could not be.

BUT, as Carroad worked, as the beam moved, as the power was raised or lowered, so did the voice, though always the same in tone and speed, change in phrase. Carroad had slowed the speed of detection, and individual words could be heard. And it was obvious that the age level of the speaker was fluctuating. Yet, throughout the swiftly leaping sentences, there was a sameness, an identity of personality. Sometimes, it was a baby just learning the language. At other times, it was an adolescent or young boy.

"Well, man, what is it?" bellowed the Secretary.

The mysterious voice had struck sparks off even his iron nerves.

Jane answered for her husband.

"I'll tell you what it is. It's the voice of my unborn son."

"Jane, you're insane!" said Carroad.

"No, I'm not, though I wish I were."

194

"God, he's at the window!" boomed the voice. *"And he has a knife! What can I do? What can I do?"*

"Turn that off until I get through talking," said Jane. "Then, you can listen again and see if what I'm saying isn't true."

Carroad stood like a statue, his hand extended towards the toggle switch but not reaching it. Cramer reached past him and flicked the switch.

"James," she said, speaking slowly and with difficulty. "You want to make robots out of everyone. Except, of course, yourself and the State's leaders. But what if I told you that you don't have to do that? That Nature or God or whatever you care to call the Creator, has anticipated you? And done so by several billion years?

"No, don't look at me that way. You'll see what I mean. Now, look. The only one whose thoughts you could possible have tapped is our son. Yet, it's impossible for an unborn baby to have a knowledge of speech. Nevertheless, you heard thoughts, originated by a boy, seeming to run from the first years of speech up to those of an adolescent. You have to admit that, even if you don't know what it means.

"Well, I do."

Tears running down her cheeks, choking, she said, "Maybe. I see the truth where you don't because I'm closer to my baby. It's part of me. Oh, I know you'll say I'm talking like a silly woman. Maybe. Anyway, I think that what we've heard means that we—all of humanity without exception—are machines. Not steel and electrical robots, no, but still machines of flesh, engines whose behavior, motives, and very thoughts, conscious or unconscious, spring from the playing of protein tapes in our brains."

"What the hell are you talking about?" said Carroad.

"If I'm right, we are in hell," she said. "Through no fault or choice of ours. Listen to me before you shut your ears because you don't want to hear, can't hear.

MEMORIES are not recordings of what has happened in our past. Nor do we act as we will. We speak and behave according to our 'memories,' which are not recorded *after* the fact. They're recorded *before* the fact. Our actions are such because our memories tell us to do such. Each of us is set like a clockwork doll. Oh, not independently, but intermeshed, working together, synchronized as a masterclock or masterplan decrees.

"And, all this time, we think we are creatures of free will and chance. But we do not know there isn't such a thing as chance, that all is plotted and foretold, and we are sliding over the world, through time, in predetermined grooves. We, body and mind, are walking recordings. Deep within our cells, a molecular needle follows the grooves, and we follow the needle.

"Somehow, this experiment has ripped the cover from the machine, showed us the tape, stimulated it into working long before it was supposed to."

Suddenly, she began laughing. And, between laughing and gasping, she said, "What am I saying? It can't be an accident. If we have discovered that we're puppets, it's because we're supposed to do so."

"Jane, Jane!" said Carroad, "You're wild, wild! Foolish woman's intuition! You're supposed to be a scientist! Stop talking! Control yourself!"

The Secretary bellowed for silence, and, after a minute, succeeded. He said, "Mrs. Carroad, please continue. We'll get to the bottom of this."

He, too, was pale and wide-eyed. But he had not gotten to his position by refusing to attack.

She ordered Cramer to run the beam again over the previous areas. He was to speed up the process and slow down only when she so directed.

The result was a stream of unintelligibility's. Occasionally, when Cramer slowed Cervus at a gesture from Jane, it broke into a rate of speech they could understand. And, when it did, they trembled. They could not deny that they were speeding over the life thoughts of a growing male named James Carroad, Junior. Even at the velocity at which they traveled and the great jumps in time that the machine had to make in order to cover the track quickly, they could tell that.

AFTER an hour, Jane had Cramer cut off the voice. In the silence, looking at the white and sweating men, she said, "We are getting close to the end. Should we go on?"

Hoarsely, the Secretary shouted, "This is a hoax! I can prove it must be! It's impossible! If we carry the seeds of predeterminism within us, and yet, as now, we discover how to foresee what we shall do, why can't we change the future?"

"I don't know, Mr. Secretary," said Jane. "We'll find out—in time. I can tell you this. If anyone is preset to foretell the future, he'll do so. If no one is, then the problem will go begging. It all depends on Whoever wound us up."

"That's blasphemy!" howled the Secretary, a man noted for his belligerent atheism. But he did not order the voice to stop after Jane told Cramer to start the machine up again.

Cramer ran Cervus at full speed. The words became a staccato of incomprehensibility; the oscilloscope, an almost solid blur. Flickers of blackness told of broad jumps forward, and then the wild intertwined lightning resumed.

Suddenly, the oscilloscope went blank, and the voice was silent.

Jane Carroad said, "Backtrack a little, Jason. And then run it forward at normal speed."

James Carroad had been standing before her, rigid, a figure seemingly made of white metal, his face almost as white as his uniform. Abruptly, he broke into fluidity and lurched out of the laboratory. His motions were broken; his shouts, broken also.

"Won't stay to listen...rot...mysticism...believe this...go insane! Mean...no control...no control..."

And his voice was lost as the door closed behind him.

Jane said, "I don't want to hear this, Jason. But..."

Instantly, the voice boomed, *"God, he's at the window! And he has a knife! What can I do? What can I do? Father, father, I'm your son! He knows it, he knows it, yet he's going to kill me. The window! He's breaking it! Oh, Lord, he's been locked up for nineteen years, ever since he shot and killed my mother and all those men and I was born a Caesarian and I didn't know he'd escape and still want to kill me, though they told me that's all he talked about, raving mad, and..."*

THE END

If you've enjoyed this book, you will not want to miss these terrific titles...

ARMCHAIR SCI-FI, FANTASY, & HORROR DOUBLE NOVELS, $12.95 each

D-1 **THE GALAXY RAIDERS** by William P. McGivern
SPACE STATION #1 by Frank Belknap Long

D-2 **THE PROGRAMMED PEOPLE** by Jack Sharkey
SLAVES OF THE CRYSTAL BRAIN by William Carter Sawtelle

D-3 **YOU'RE ALL ALONE** by Fritz Leiber
THE LIQUID MAN by Bernard C. Gilford

D-4 **CITADEL OF THE STAR LORDS** by Edmund Hamilton
VOYAGE TO ETERNITY by Milton Lesser

D-5 **IRON MEN OF VENUS** by Don Wilcox
THE MAN WITH ABSOLUTE MOTION by Noel Loomis

D-6 **WHO SOWS THE WIND...** by Rog Phillips
THE PUZZLE PLANET by Robert A. W. Lowndes

D-7 **PLANET OF DREAD** by Murray Leinster
TWICE UPON A TIME by Charles L. Fontenay

D-8 **THE TERROR OUT OF SPACE** by Dwight V. Swain
QUEST OF THE GOLDEN APE by Ivar Jorgensen and Adam Chase

D-9 **SECRET OF MARRACOTT DEEP** by Henry Slesar
PAWN OF THE BLACK FLEET by Mark Clifton.

D-10 **BEYOND THE RINGS OF SATURN** by Robert Moore Williams
A MAN OBSESSED by Alan E. Nourse

ARMCHAIR SCIENCE FICTION CLASSICS, $12.95 each

C-1 **THE GREEN MAN**
by Harold M. Sherman

C-2 **A TRACE OF MEMORY**
By Keith Laumer

C-3 **INTO PLUTONIAN DEPTHS**
by Stanton A. Coblentz

ARMCHAIR MASTERS OF SCIENCE FICTION SERIES, $16.95 each

M-1 **MASTERS OF SCIENCE FICTION, Vol. One**
Bryce Walton—"Dark of the Moon" and other tales

M-2 **MASTERS OF SCIENCE FICTION, Vol. Two**
Jerome Bixby: "One Way Street" and other tales

If you've enjoyed this book, you will not want to miss these terrific titles…

ARMCHAIR SCI-FI, FANTASY, & HORROR DOUBLE NOVELS, $12.95 each

D-21   **EMPIRE OF EVIL** by Robert Arnette
THE SIGN OF THE TIGER by Alan E. Nourse & J. A. Meyer

D-22   **OPERATION SQUARE PEG** by Frank Belknap Long
ENCHANTRESS OF VENUS by Leigh Brackett

D-23   **THE LIFE WATCH** by Lester Del Rey
CREATURES OF THE ABYSS by Murray Leinster

D-24   **LEGION OF LAZARUS** by Edmond Hamilton
STAR HUNTER by Andre Norton

D-25   **EMPIRE OF WOMEN** by John Fletcher
ONE OF OUR CITIES IS MISSING by Irving Cox

D-26   **THE WRONG SIDE OF PARADISE** by Raymond F. Jones
THE INVOLUNTARY IMMORTALS by Rog Phillips

D-27   **EARTH QUARTER** by Damon Knight
ENVOY TO NEW WORLDS by Keith Laumer

D-28   **SLAVES TO THE METAL HORDE** by Milton Lesser
HUNTERS OUT OF TIME by Joseph E. Kelleam

D-29   **RX JUPITER SAVE US** by Ward Moore
BEWARE THE USURPERS by Geoff St. Reynard

D-30   **SECRET OF THE SERPENT** by Don Wilcox
CRUSADE ACROSS THE VOID by Dwight V. Swain

ARMCHAIR SCIENCE FICTION CLASSICS, $12.95 each

C-7   **THE SHAVER MYSTERY, pt. 1**
by Richard S. Shaver

C-8   **THE SHAVER MYSTERY, pt. 2**
by Richard S. Shaver

C-9   **MURDER IN SPACE**
by David V. Reed

ARMCHAIR MASTERS OF SCIENCE FICTION SERIES, $16.95 each

M-3   **MASTERS OF SCIENCE FICTION, Vol. Three**
Robert Sheckley, "The Perfect Woman" and other tales

M-4   **MASTERS OF SCIENCE FICTION, Vol. Four**
Mack Reynolds, "Stowaway" and other tales

If you've enjoyed this book, you will not want to miss these terrific titles…

ARMCHAIR SCI-FI & HORROR DOUBLE NOVELS, $12.95 each

ARMCHAIR SCIENCE FICTION CLASSICS, $12.95 each

ARMCHAIR SCIENCE FICTION & HORROR GEMS SERIES, $12.95 each